T0171555

THE TICK TRIBE

ERIKA LOGAN

BALBOA.
PRESS

A DIVISION OF HAY HOUSE

Balboa Press books may be ordered through booksellers or by contacting:

Balboa Press
A Division of Hay House
1663 Liberty Drive
Bloomington, IN 47403
www.balboapress.com.au
1-(877) 407-4847

ISBN: 978-1-4525-0712-5 (sc)
ISBN: 978-1-4525-0713-2 (e)

Printed in the United States of America

Balboa Press rev. date: 10/25/2012

For Reilly and Stella, my precious brother and sister

. . . also for Jane, with much love, gratitude, and admiration.

Many thanks to my mum, Logan, for a lifetime of love, support and encouragement. Thank you to Tin for being you and for completing our beautiful family. Thank you to Zyggii for Malachite and all the other times you helped get me through my writer's block. Thank you to Annemarie and Tammy for *Tuesdays*, the laughter was essential. Also to my partner who patiently waited, quietly encouraged and always, without fail, believed in me.

A very special thanks to all the amazing students at Fitzroy Primary School, especially Dylan; whose love of reading inspired me to write this book in the first place.

CONTENTS

CHAPTER 1

Movement

IT WAS TIME.

Lowky uncurled himself from what he now realised was a very hard and uneven surface. He didn't know how long he had been there—at least a day, maybe two. He hadn't eaten, and as soon as he started to move, he understood the reason for the uncurling. He was starving! His mum always used to say, "You're hungry Lowky; *not* starving." He wanted to cry, but a little internal voice said, *No, Lowky, it's time.* The voice was gentle and warm, and Lowky attempted a smile as he stretched his legs. This was harder than he'd expected. He had been curled up for so long that even though his mind wanted to move, his body did not. He tried again. His limbs slowly remembered what they were supposed to do, and before long he was standing, slightly crouched, in what used to be his living room.

The house was half there and half gone. The living room was mainly standing; only the front corner had collapsed. To the south of that, the dining room and kitchen were badly shaken but also okay. The rest of the house was destroyed. The front of the house and the street it was connected to faced west. These had completely collapsed, and from what Lowky could see, had been reduced to rubble.

Lowky hobbled to the kitchen. The smell was overpowering. It was the smell of food starting to rot, slimy rot! Luckily for Lowky, he had nothing in his stomach to throw up. He did manage, however, to dry-retch all the way to the centre of the kitchen. Most of the contents of the cupboards were on the floor, so he grabbed a dented can of baked beans and attempted to run to the back door.

As he hobbled towards the yard, he imagined he must look like the Elephant man. "I am not an animal," he giggled as he balanced on a small pile of rubble that used to be the neighbour's shed. Hungrily he pulled the ring pull on the baked beans and used his fingers to shovel them into his mouth. *Big mistake*, he thought. He had had nothing to drink, and the beans turned into a semi-set cement. His stomach reacted to this substance and he started to heave even before he tried to swallow.

He looked back at the kitchen. *No chance those pipes are working,* he thought as he spat the baked beans into the rubble next to him. He looked around but couldn't imagine finding water anywhere. He remembered the stash of lemonade his mum kept for her after-work pick-me-ups. This was always mixed with a large splash of vodka, but she thought Lowky didn't know. The thought hit him immediately: *Oh no! Back to the slimy rot.*

The lemonade had been shaken out of the cupboard like most of the other contents. He could see it from what used to be the back door. He steadied himself, took a deep breath, and hobbled as fast as he could to the can of lemonade. His stiff body had loosened up a bit, so it didn't take as long as the first trip. He was weak though, and the lack of food, water, and now oxygen made his head spin and his knees shake. *Ohhh,* he groaned when he realised he would have to take a breath. He held on to a solid, but shaken, bench frame, grabbed the lemonade, took a disgustingly deep breath, and wobbled, cried, and heaved all the way to the back door.

The lemonade was sweet and warm. He gulped down three huge mouthfuls, but his body rejected it. *Gross,* he thought, as it cascaded down the rubble next to the baked beans. It was then that he remembered a documentary he had seen about people who should have died but didn't. When they were finally rescued, they were given only tiny sips of water. At the time he had thought this was some kind of cruel joke or a feature of the documentary to make it more interesting. Now he knew better.

He sat back down on the pile of rubble and perched between a rock and a piece of tin. He took a tiny sip of lemonade. This time his body gratefully accepted it. It took Lowky what seemed like forever to absorb only a quarter of the can. It had probably lasted an hour, but it made him aware that without a clock or a schedule, time became irrelevant. At that moment, he had nowhere to go, nothing to do, and no reason for living. He decided not to cry as he had had enough trouble drinking the lemonade. What would be the point of wasting it? He quickly changed his focus back to the baked beans.

I can do this, he thought, *just take it one bean at a time*. This worked, and after what seemed like another eternity Lowky had eaten about ten beans. He was full and quenched. He was safe and unhurt. He was scared and lonely but somewhere deep inside he was glad to be alive.

It was a sunny day, hot and dry, which was unusual for Melbourne. He lived on one of the hottest continents on Earth, yet the town he lived in rarely finished a day without seeing clouds and rain. The flipside of this was that a day rarely finished without some sun as well. Melbourne was known for having four seasons in one day, and unless you were a tourist you always carried a set of clothes that could be changed as easily as the weather.

On this day the sun was nice and he wished it would stay that way so he could defrost his bones and rehabilitate his muscles. And it did.

Lowky hadn't moved over the last day or two. He knew his mother and sister were dead in the next room and he had stayed there paralysed as he slipped in and out of his grief. He had heard some noise in the surrounding area—mainly screaming and crying but also helping and saving. On four occasions he had heard groups of people calling out for any lost or hurt people. He had remained perfectly still, not daring to breathe because he did not want to be found—which he knew would require a lot of planning.

He had heard very little movement during the night, so that would be the best time to do any noisy or outdoor work. He suddenly realised where he was, sitting high on some rubble, in the middle of the day like a lighthouse just begging to be seen. He quickly slid off his perch and hid in the dining room. He sat silently behind the only solid piece of wall he could find. Lowky had to get organised.

It was time.

CHAPTER 2

A . . . B . . . C

OVERNIGHT, Lowky had come up with three ideas. His first plan was not his favourite. It went something like this:

Plan A: Stay put and do nothing. It would mean staying hidden and raiding shops and houses for food at night, but this would be difficult with the police and SES looking for survivors. However, Lowky was starting to think the area had been completely cut off because he had only heard loud movement about once a day. He heard the movement of individuals more often. But the noise that came from search groups rarely buzzed through the air.

What scared Lowky most about this plan was that he didn't want to risk ending up in an orphanage or with some random family—or worse still, some random, toothless aunt or uncle he only saw, by force, at Christmas or funerals. No, plan A was definitely out.

Plan B: Find Aunty Edie. She was Lowky's mum's sister. She was always there: every camping trip, every celebration, every tragedy, every triumph, every adventure, every complication—always. If Edie was alive, she would be looking for her sister. Edie was their nearest and dearest, and her daughter, Ales, was like a sister to Lowky.

Lowky allowed himself to wonder for a second. *Was Edie alive? Had she escaped?* He believed she had. She was ingenious and essential. She was like a Swiss army knife: when she was around, anything was possible.

This reminded Lowky of Plan C: Spargo Creek. Lowky had been there with Edie, Ales, and his mum on many occasions. On the first occasion, Lowky had been five. That was by no means their first camping trip. Camping with Aunt Edie had been a monthly occurrence. A tradition, if you like. Ales had always been a go-getter, and on that particular morning, she had already salvaged some bread, cheese, olives, shallots, and tomatoes.

Lowky had crawled out of bed and grabbed the cast-iron toastie maker from its usual place under the bus. He'd tossed it into the fire to heat up and then wandered down the path to the abundant vegetable garden. It was mid-autumn, and at the far right of the garden he found a thick patch of juicy basil. He picked a few sprigs and headed back up the path.

Ales had taken the toastie iron out of the fire and was stoking it with small sticks. She was two years younger than Lowky, but he felt absolutely no concern for her safety. This was the life they had always lived. Spending endless months on the road, their parents picking what seemed to be an endless variety of fruit and vegetables. They had lived out of tents, cabins, or sheds for most of their lives. They were not "cotton wool children" with "helicopter parents." They were more "Bob and Bindi" types. This made him laugh, as they had regularly joked about the children of Steve Irwin—the great "Crocodile Hunter." In fact, this lifestyle continued for Lowky until he started school, and he didn't do that until he was almost seven.

That morning long ago Lowky had started preparing the toasties. He was an expert. He knew everybody's preferences, and nobody bothered to get out of bed until they could smell the fire and the coffee. He filled up the billy and placed it on the fire. He put four teaspoons of coffee—Ethiopian dark blend, his mum's favourite—into the plunger.

"Hey, Lowky, wait! I just found mushrooms and feta." Ales's voice still had baby overtones, but her vocabulary was quite extraordinary.

It wasn't long before Lowky's mum got up. "Good morning, good morning, good morning," she chanted as she stumbled blurry-eyed out of the bus. Lowky and Ales were never quite sure who she was talking to, but they said good morning anyway.

"It smells good," she said soothingly as she wrapped her arms around Lowky. The water bubbled on the fire, and she searched for a long stick before she approached it. She was talented, and like an acrobat she managed to simultaneously pick up the billy and turn the toastie. She filled the plunger with steaming water but couldn't be bothered waiting for it to infuse and pushed the filter too quickly to the bottom. She poured the coffee and sat on a log as Lowky climbed into her lap.

"How'd you sleep, honey?" she inquired.

"Great." He beamed. He didn't stay long; he could hear the cheese in the toasty sizzling and wasting into the fire. He jumped up to save them but his mum pulled him back for one more quick squeeze.

The toasties came out of the fire with the perfect amount of crispiness, and Lowky piled them on a plate so he could make the next batch. No one touched them. It wasn't that they weren't hungry, and it wasn't that they weren't delicious; it was tradition. The next two he made were for his mum and himself. She loved extra, extra cheese. Lowky looked back now and wished he had added more of everything: more cheese, more olives, more love. Ales made two hot chocolates, and by the time the next batch of toasties was ready, Edie was up and out of the bus. Her timing was always perfect. It was uncanny!

So there they were a motley crew in their pyjamas and boots. They grabbed their breakfast, and without a word headed towards the dam. The property was amazing, and when they stayed there, they wanted for nothing. Not only did it have shade, it had a veggie patch, chickens, a cow, a calf, a dam, and an abundant amount of wood for the fire. There was also a little mud brick cabin, which they called the shed. It had a bed and mainly stored camping equipment. Occasionally Lowky's mum or aunt Edie would go in there and come out with some random item, such as a pick or a fly swatter. It was never locked and rarely used.

After breakfast, they all walked to the dam for a swim/bath. The sun was just starting to leave rays of speckled heat through the trees. They washed themselves in mud (which believe it or not is quite effective). Edie joked that she had just spent three hundred dollars at a spa in Melbourne getting a mud wrap. She said that's why the words "hippy" and "yuppie" were so similar.

Eventually Lowky's mum and Edie settled on the grass in the sun while Lowky and Ales did tricks in the water. They used the pipe from the water pump to swing and twist like circus performers. They could have stayed there all day, but eventually the adults would want for coffee and they'd all head back dripping and laughing.

While the adults made what was the beginning of an endless stream of coffee and pancakes, the kids would sneak off and drink sweet, fresh water straight from the water tank. Their lips would wrap around the faucet as they tried to drink at the rate that the water left the tank. Lowky's mum didn't like this and would yell at them about the waste of water and the earth and blah, blah, blah.

Lowky snapped back to reality. He made a mental note to find water, matches, and the toastie iron.

Lowky pondered his options for quite a while and decided it was a choice between plan B and plan C. Ultimately, though, he knew he could do nothing until he tried to find Aunt Edie. And if he couldn't find her, then maybe he could find Spargo Creek. It was at least a hundred kilometres away, but it had everything and he prided himself on being a self-sufficient, capable warrior.

In fact, he was so independent that he once persuaded his mum to let him stay with an Aboriginal tribe. They were on one of their many Australian bush adventures, and his mum was due to work on a farm, fixing fences. Lowky hated those jobs; he would be left all day to entertain himself. At the same time he had to be where she "could see him." Trapped but free—the worst possible scenario.

Lowky begged and pleaded and begged some more. He talked to the tribal elder, and although the man laughed heartily, he said Lowky could stay. Lowky's mum easily agreed, and off she went to her job with complete faith that the universe would protect her son. Most people would have been horrified by a child having this much freedom, but not them—that was how they rolled.

Lowky slept happily by the fire and when he woke, the elder had taken him deep into the bush to initiate him with a smorgasbord of bugs.

Lowky was jolted from this memory by a noise; he pushed himself deeper into the corner of the crumpled living room. He waited anxiously... nothing! He breathed a sigh of relief and went back to the comfort of his memories.

There was no doubt Lowky could survive in Spargo Creek, and if he got there, he would almost be guaranteed food, shelter, and water. Yes, Spargo Creek was defiantly an option.

CHAPTER 3

Dog

Lowky had a plan, and now he needed to formulate a plan within a plan. He had started to get organised on the day of his uncurling by taping the curtains up where the windows used to be. Then he started a fire in the living room using scrap wood from the broken furniture and collected everything warm from the coat rack, using the assortment of items to create a bed.

Lowky rebuilt the fire on the ashes from the night before. The house was built on a cement slab, so the fire was easily contained. He used some kindling from outside and the remainder of the kitchen chairs and coat rack to get the fire blazing. Once the fire had settled, he put on a pot of water, reached into the pocket of an oversized jacket, and pulled out a camomile teabag. He counted the bags. Five left. He had never liked camomile tea but now it was like a treasure, a special gift. Once the water boiled, he poured his tea and again reflected on Ales's toasties.

That would be nice, he thought. The only problem was, he had no bread, no cheese, no tomatoes—no toasties. *Such is life,* he giggled. *Good old Ned Kelly—what would he do now?*

Lowky got up and looked out the window. He had left a slight gap so the smoke could escape. The house had a large auto-mechanic shop at the back, which meant the view straight out was a brick wall. Next door was the corner store, which meant the view to the right was also a brick wall. The house on the left had a large shed with a fig tree in the far left corner. So this view was a tin wall with a smear of green. Lowky had spent four years looking at that green smear, watching it dance in the breeze. Lowky's mum initially hated the backyard. "How will I connect with nature'" she had droned. Eventually she grew to love it, appreciating the privacy it created, and she realised nature was everywhere. Plus, it was all they could afford.

Over the last few days, the privacy had been a blessing for Lowky. It meant smoke could escape from the living room without anyone from the street noticing. It also meant he could spend some time outside in the sun. He only did this in the morning, as it was too dangerous with the hustle-bustle daytime might bring.

In reality there was little hustle-bustle. But now that he had a plan, he couldn't afford to get caught. Three days earlier there had been noise in the street, mainly crying and panic, but now there was no life on the ground, only in the air. Once he had uncurled himself he had noticed that once the sun was up, so were the search-and-rescue helicopters. Hiding a bit of smoke from a fire was manageable. Hiding his eleven-year-old self would be much more difficult.

It had already been one day since the uncurling. Lowky woke up early on the second day, but it was already late for what he had planned. He had decided there was no point waiting anymore. Waiting for what? The earthquake had claimed his mother and sister, and although he didn't want to accept it, they were not coming back.

"I need water," he mumbled. It was early spring, and the land around him was twisted, crumbled, and damp. He climbed out of the frame of the stoic back door. He moved quietly away from his family and headed down what used to be Pyjama Lane. He headed left towards Matilda's house. Matilda was his best friend, and as he walked he wondered why he had never told her that. They had met when they were six. Their birthdays were exactly six months apart. Lowky was just about to turn seven, and his mum had decided it was time for him to start school. She hated the idea of it, but she sold their bus and rented the house in the city. Of course Lowky's mum couldn't give it up completely. She replaced the bus with a smaller van, which she decked out with a bed just big enough for three. Just after she had enrolled Lowky in school she found out she was pregnant. Nine months later Lowky was blessed with Tushita, his baby sister. They continued to camp and travel whenever the opportunity arose. Which was often.

Matilda had lived in her house, number three Pyjama Lane, since she was born. Her parents had bought the dingy, rundown house when Matilda's mum was pregnant with her. It was far from their dream home, but it was what they could afford. They had planned on selling and upgrading when they could, but once they started making it their own, they just couldn't leave. It was nothing like it had been when Lowky first met them. He could only imagine how it had been when they had first arrived. They were always working on it, building this or fixing that. Lowky looked at the destruction around him and knew all their years of hard work had been in vain.

Pyjama Lane was tiny, but it was hard work getting to Matilda's only two houses away. A tree had collapsed on the front of the house. The other rooms at the front were flattened, but it seemed that part of the kitchen and bedrooms were standing. He called out to Matilda, but there was no response, and he didn't want to make too much noise. He attempted to move closer, but it was obvious he would only be able to reach those rooms from Overhill Road. He couldn't move forward because of the tree blocking his way, and a small split in the ground had totally cut off the lane ahead. He decided to turn back and try to access Overhill Road from Koves Street at the other end of the lane. In that direction the lane had held up pretty well. The old bluestones laneways of the inner city had just made it out to Thornbury and Pyjama Lane was one of them. It wasn't really called Pyjama Lane; in fact, it had no name. Initially the houses had stretched all the way from Overhill Road to the lane at the back, but as the city developed, they cut off the front of the houses and turned them into shops. Now in 2012, Overhill Road was quite a thriving shopping strip, and the houses at the back were unknown to many of the locals. Matilda and Lowky had informally named the lane because they were always running to each other's houses in their pyjamas. Their parents had also become fast friends, and they often did a PJ dash early in the morning to borrow coffee or milk. Anyway, the name had caught on, and they had all called it that from the time it was invented.

There was only one small split at the bottom of the lane, between Lowky's house and the corner store. It continued across the lane to the auto-mechanic's. The split was only about a metre wide, but it had enough strength to split the garage in two and send it crashing into the centre. The split was about two metres deep, and Lowky could have climbed into it and out again, but he took a run and easily cleared the gap.

From the other side, Lowky could see the corner store. The house at the back had been flattened but the store itself was partially standing. Lowky couldn't pass over the rubble to get there. He was trapped on PJ Lane. *Maybe I can approach it from the street on the other side,* he thought. It was hard to see very far ahead on his street, which looked like a war zone.

Lowky managed to get past the mangled fence and onto Koves Street. Two power poles had fallen and the road was covered in power lines. Lowky knew this meant danger but couldn't remember why. Was it that he couldn't touch them? Or was it that he couldn't be near them at all? He was about two metres away from the closest one, and the thought made him freeze. From where he was standing he could see the coffee shop on the other side of the road.

Out of nowhere a dog turned the corner. Lowky tried to yell out, but all he could manage was a surprised, "Stay." The dog didn't hear him and kept coming, oblivious to any danger. Lowky shut his eyes and covered his head as the dog walked unaware towards the power lines. Lowky covered his ears. He was scared to look. He didn't want to see what would happen. This was not the world he knew, and he felt overwhelmed by his fear. He had no idea how to get to Overhill Road, no idea if Matilda was alive, and no way of finding out. He was suddenly snapped out of his thoughts by the big wet lick from a very lucky dog. Lowky beamed. It was the first good thing to happen to him in what seemed like forever. In fact, it was the first real smile he had managed since the earthquake, and his lips were so dry that a split in the corner of his mouth started to bleed.

It was then that he noticed the water tank in the yard of the corner store. Of course this was not the first time he had seen it. He had seen it hundreds of times before, but as he looked at it now, perched on its stand like the Leaning Tower of Pisa, he was surprised by its existence. There was some debris between him and the tank, but he thought he could manage it. The idea of water had never been so appealing. In fact, it had never been appealing at all.

"Stay," he croaked to the dog as he started to climb the buckled fence. The dog ran ahead of him and waited on the other side.

"I said stay!" he croaked again, and the dog just panted and waited. Once Lowky scrambled across the fence, he had to climb the wall of the house and into the yard. It was from this position that Lowky could see that not only had the house been flattened, so had the whole back wall of the shop. Lowky could see right through the corner store to Overhill Road at the front. He didn't want to think what he would find inside. He had known the Wangs and their children for as long as he has known Matilda, and although they weren't close, he couldn't bear finding them inside.

He turned away and climbed down the wall to the base of the water tank. The tank was damaged, but only halfway down. As he half-slid and half-climbed down the damaged wall, he tapped on the side of the tank to find it half full. He climbed towards the tap and took a deep breath as he held on to the handle. The tap seemed undamaged but the handle wouldn't budge. Lowky placed himself precariously on a hunk of bricks that was closest to the tap. The dog looked on enthusiastically. He panted a couple of times, and Lowky realised the dog was thirsty too. He lined himself up with the tank and the tap. Not only was the tank wobbling, so were the bricks he was standing on.

One ... two ... three ... he pulled with all his might, and to his surprise the handle moved easily and sent him tumbling down the pile of mess to the ground below. He knew immediately he had hurt his arm but he didn't care. The only thing he could think about was the precious water. He needed water.

He scrambled back up towards the tap. The dog was already there lapping up any water he could salvage. Lowky wrapped his lips around the faucet and gulped down mouthful after mouthful. He drank like this until he thought he was going to burst. The water was the sweetest, purest water he had ever tasted. He later found out that the water was filthy, putrid, but at the time he didn't notice. Lowky looked around for something he could use as a bowl for the dog and found a torn and dented piece of tin.

"This will do fine, won't it, boy?" he said as he filled it with water and placed it on the uneven surface. It leaked a little but the dog was drinking at a very fast rate. Finally, after Lowky had filled the tin several times, the dog sat, satisfied. They both smiled, happy but miserable, looking perplexed as they stared into the corner store.

"Okay," Lowky said as he turned to the dog. "Good luck." He smiled as he started crawling towards the back wall. He was scared to stand in case his foot got caught in one of the endless crevasses.

If Lowky had paid attention earlier he wouldn't have had to crawl through the store. He would have seen the dog standing directly on a power line. He would have realised the power to the city was destroyed or cut off or something. But fear had made him close his eyes, and now here he was scrambling towards what he hoped would be some edible food and Matilda.

Even crawling was treacherous, as every bit of brick wobbled. As Lowky was trying to secure the next handhold, the dog trotted past him, crawled under a beam, and waited patiently on what used to be the counter. He panted twice before sniffing around.

"Careful!" Lowky called as he quickened his pace, and before long he found himself on all fours, on the counter, with the dog. Lowky smiled. "If you insist on staying, I'll have to give you a name."

The dog lifted his head, and out of his mouth popped a banana lolly.

"Oh, you're good!" Lowky giggled. "I love them." Lowky looked down at at least a hundred lollies. He picked up three and carefully cleaned them of glass and debris before stuffing them into his mouth. Lowky and the dog were in heaven until they were bought back to reality by a very loud creak.

"Come on, dog," he yelled as he grabbed a handful of lollies and stuffed them into his pockets. Then he twisted, ducked, and slid out the other side of the corner store and into the street beyond. Of course the dog was there first, waiting patiently. They both looked back at the store, and although it had shifted a little, to Lowky's surprise it was still mostly standing.

"Basically, dog, that's our only chance of food."

The dog just got up and negotiated the rubble as he headed in the direction of Matilda's. Of course Lowky followed. He didn't know if the store would still be standing when he got back, but "Dog" was right. They had to see if Matilda was okay.

Overhill Road was split and crumpled like everything else. Dog didn't seem to notice and plodded forward as if it was any other day. It was natural to follow. Dog was smart on his feet and Lowky was glad he was there. The dog took the easiest route for four legs. Lowky had to negotiate every step—*heavy-footed like an elephant*, his mum used to say, and she was right; he was no Billy Elliot.

Lowky and Dog didn't know it yet but a new family was about to be born, and they were the first two members.

CHAPTER 4

Cloud

MATILDA's house was basically destroyed; maybe one or two rooms in the middle had survived. It was impossible to get to them, so Lowky called her name.

"Matilda, Matilda!" He tried to climb over part of the rubble, terrified he would disturb something underneath. The dog got to the top of a small mound and sniffed around. Again Lowky called out Matilda's name. He also started shouting the names of her parents: "Matilda! Madra, Monte! Matilda, Matilda!"

After a long time of listening for nothing, Lowky sat defeated on a pile of Matilda's house. The dog was sniffing in an uninterested manner around the rubble on Overhill Road. Lowky noticed that the light was fading, and he started to head back down towards the store. One lonesome cloud had come in and floated across the sun, and Lowky felt defeated. He knew he had to get to the rooms in the middle, but it just seemed so dangerous. It was as if there would always be a cloud over his head and a storm in his heart. The dog seemed to sense the desperation and slightly hung his head. They both stumbled back down the street. There was, however, one ray of sunshine: food!

CHAPTER 5

Inventory

THEY sat outside the corner store as if waiting for it to fall. It was a huge risk, but inside were treasures of all descriptions. Lowky couldn't stop visualising the lollies he'd seen earlier. Neither could Dog.

It was Dog who made the first move. Just like that he got up and headed towards the gap in the collapsed door. He paused and looked at Lowky as if to say, *Are you coming?*

Lowky got up and headed gratefully towards the door. He followed the dog until they were both back on the counter and looking around at the loot. It was almost exciting, a daydream adventure where a boy and his dog get trapped in a lolly shop. At that very moment, Lowky and the dog grabbed a lolly and shared it with deliberate mindfulness.

When they looked around, they realised the inside was tangled and torn. Lowky went into leader mode; he grabbed the closest things to him (three cans of condensed milk) and moved towards the backyard. As he moved he cleared a tiny path ready for the next trip. Dog followed.

The main area of the store was wide and open, with paper stands and ice cream fridges. The counter was big and wooden with a glass front that housed layer upon layer of sweet delights. Lowky wondered how much pocket money he had spent here and how many hours he had whiled away looking into those displays.

The counter was now completely flat. It had collapsed on itself, and most of the riches underneath were buried in its weight. Some random lollies had been blown clear and were lying on the floor in the glass. That was Lowky's first mission. *This store will not fall until I've captured the lollies,* he thought, laughing. He tried to make the dog stay outside but he learnt very quickly that Dog did his own thing.

Lowky collected whatever could be collected: baked beans, coconut cream, cereal, and bottled water. It was on his fifth trip that he decided he needed a system. They needed some essentials before everything collapsed.

The back end of the shop had three standalone selves full of random groceries. This area was very unstable and all the shelving, lighting, and advertising had ended up in a heap under some concrete from the ceiling. He had managed to get some things from the front of the pile but would need to plan carefully to get the things at the back. He would need dog food, flour, and lighters.

"Strategy, Dog, strategy," he whispered as he crawled back into the ever-creaking building. He remembered the basic layout of the shelves, and the dog food was at the back near the deodorants and soaps. That, of course, was the aisle that had been completely smashed by the concrete ceiling. The other side of the shelf was slightly accessible, so Lowky got on his stomach and crawled under the first section. There were chips strewn all over the bottom of the aisle. Lowky tried to kick them out with his feet but everything wobbled. He also found a packet of Tim-Tams. He slid forward and sifted through the chaos until he finally found dog food: three dented cans and some dry food. He managed to push the cans down to his feet, but as he moved, the shelves swayed to and fro. Instead he had to hold on and wriggle out backward! He was petrified when everything swayed as he slid out into a small clearing.

Dog was waiting. They weaved their way outside and piled the dog food with the rest of the supplies.

"The lighters should be near the counter somewhere," Lowky told Dog. He went back to the shelving, and using only his hands he scooped out everything he could reach. Lowky was weak with the stress of it and decided it was the most he could manage. He took everything outside, and on his way found the lighters and some plastic bags.

The pile outside filled three plastic bags, which was more than enough. Dog led the way, finding the quickest and kindest route. Lowky was glad he didn't have to explain this feeling, and he was glad he wasn't alone. *I must give you a name,* he thought.

Once Lowky got home he knew he had to get organised. It had been four days since the earthquake and he was scared that his chances of finding Aunt Edie were slipping away. He had temporarily set himself up, but that didn't help him with his long-term plan. It was time to take some action.

The only part of the house that didn't smell yet was the lounge room with the fire pit. He decided to collect all the edible food from the house and carry it in there. This took forever. It must have been quite a sight as Lowky successfully faced the decay over and over again. He was so relieved when he had finally made the last trip and closed the unhinged door. He had found two more cans of lemonade, and now that his stomach had adapted, he drank them quickly. Lowky decided to make a list.

From the store
2 cans of dog food
2 cans of cat food
¾ bag dry dog food
3 cans of condensed milk
2 cans of tomato soup
1 packet of Tim-Tams
2 packets of Vita Wheat
3 large bottles of water
2 bars of soap
3 cartons of shelf milk
9 lighters
51 assorted lollies
1 pack of plastic bags

From the house

1 can of lemonade

3 cans of baked beans

1 can of chick peas

5 cans of tomatoes

1 packet of lentils

3 packets of split peas

5 packets of pasta

1 packet of rice

½ packet corn flakes

3 muesli bars

3 jars of pasta a sauce

3 ½ packets of flour

½ jar of coffee

1 packet of mixed herbs

1 packet of Kraft deluxe macaroni and cheese

The last item on Lowky's list was his favourite. His mum had never participated in a take-away night, but macaroni and cheese was their equivalent. Lowky smiled, as he now knew what he was having for dinner.

Once Lowky and the dog had eaten, he started getting ready for the next day. He filled a small backpack that he had found on the coat stand with water, muesli bars, and Tim-Tams. His mum would have been proud of him. He smiled as he curled up on this bed of coats and waited eagerly for morning.

CHAPTER 6

Seen

THE morning came quickly for Lowky. He had already had some corn flakes when Dog finally woke up.

"Come on, Dog!" he said as he pushed over some remaining milk and cereal. He also gave him the rest of the can of milk from the night before. Dog ate both and waited patiently near the door. Lowky weaved through shortly after, and without hesitation, they both started negotiating the climb over the back fence and into the lane.

Aunt Edie's house was four blocks left and six blocks right. It was a long walk on an easy day, but on a warzone day it was near impossible. They had already been cut off twice by little splits in their path and now faced a big pile of collapsed building. It was hard to imagine what had caused this mess—clearly some sort of natural disaster—but what could do so much damage? And how far had it spread?

Lowky didn't know that just three kilometres north was a split in the earth eighty metres wide. This split ran for thousands of kilometres, and endless little splits and dips came from it. These little splits ranged in width from half a metre to twenty metres wide. The main split was so wide that everything in its path had just disappeared and everything around it was flattened beyond recognition. The massive upheaval that Lowky was dealing with was nothing compared to what was happening just to his left.

He and Dog scrambled silently for three blocks and then stopped for a drink. Lowky had found a plastic bowl at home, so he pulled it out of his bag and filled it up for his companion.

The sun was already high in the sky when they started off again. Lowky heard something and pulled the dog into a shed. In the street parallel, Lowky could hear voices. This was Edie's street, and for a second it sounded like two people, celebrating! He wanted to run over. He imagined his mum smiling and searching and he wanted to run. The terrain slowed him long enough to remember that he would not find his mum. As the grief hit him so did the idea that it could be Edie and Ales celebrating.

He scrambled a little closer but the dog held back. He listened harder to the voices. Two men. He froze! Were they search and rescue?

He grabbed Dog and tried to hide behind the wall of a building that had nothing else remaining. Unfortunately, he was too slow

"Hey, boy, are you all right?" a big man with an even larger voice called out.

"Yeah, I'm fine," Lowky shouted. "I'm here with my family, looking for my aunt." He tried to relax but his heart palpitated.

"Right," the man said suspiciously.

"Do you guys need a hand?" asked the smaller guy.

"No, thanks, we've been here for two days already. We're really just helping out now." He paused for a second. "Do you guys need a hand? I could ask my dad . . ."

"Nah, we're okay," the big one announced. "Cute dog—what's his name?"

"Shit," Lowky stammered. He thought back to when he first saw Dog at the end of his street, coming 'round the corner near . . ."Billy . . . Billy Baxter" he blurted out. "Um . . . but we mainly call him Billy . . . sometimes BB . . . except when he's in trouble, and then we call him—" Lowky's little internal voice told him to *shut up immediately.*

"Okay, then!" the man said curiously. "And what's your name?"

Lowky hesitated but couldn't think of a reason to lie, so he gave them his real name. "Lowky."

"You sure you're okay, Lowky?" the big man quizzed again.

"Yeah, I'm fine; I'm going back to my parents now. Come on D . . . Billy." Lowky tapped his leg and started to walk away.

"Well, see you, Lowky, see you, Billy Baxter." Both men turned away as they waved.

Lowky moved as quickly as possible behind the wall. He took a deep breath. "Well, Dog, it appears you have a name. Billy Baxter it is!"

Dog looked approvingly, and they sat down and rested. They stayed there for hours. Eventually the voices faded to nothing, but for hours more they stayed.

They demolished the Tim-Tams and were happy to sit in the sun for a while. Dog slept, and by mid-afternoon Lowky was ready to start moving again. He realised he was actually still blocks from the house, but the terrain seemed easier now that they had had a good rest.

Aunt Edie's street was unrecognisable. At least Lowky thought it was her street—it was so messed up he'd had to guess which house was hers. He realised how much he had relied on the visual reminders: the stained-glass fairy in the window, the pillars on the porch, and the endless pots of wildflowers and herbs.

"Aunt Edie," he called as he walked over the rubble. "Ales, Ales?" he called out over and over again.

"How could anyone survive this?" he cried. He didn't want to be left alone. Hours passed and it was late dusk by the time he sat in the rubble, his spirit crushed.

They stayed at the house overnight, sleeping in the stones with only a small fire for warmth. The next morning Lowky crawled over every centimetre of the house. Nothing remained. Throughout the search, Dog stayed loyally by his side. But Dog knew better and not once did he bark or dig or hesitate.

It was when the sun's heat really started to intensify and Lowky had drank his last sip of water that he decided the search was no use. He looked at Dog and headed back to his house.

They made no sound as they walked home via the main street. A news agency stood untouched on the flattened street. For a second everything seemed real again. Lowky stood stunned. Near the front door was a pile of newspapers, and for no apparent reason, he grabbed one. It was at that exact moment Lowky heard a sound.

"Dog, let's go!" he whispered as they stumbled comically around the back of the building.

The owners were taking a list of the damage.

He sat quietly with Dog about three metres from a broken window.

"What's the point?" she said, sounding beaten.

"We just have to wait," a man answered. He was reassuring but not convincing.

"There's no way in for miles, no accessible roads."

"We just have to wait," he repeated. "When they fix everything . . ." his voice trailed off.

"It's no use," the woman said. "What's a newsagent with no stock, no customers, no parking? We're now in a world where newsagents are no longer necessary."

Lowky picked up his paper and started to move away. He heard the girl say, "The only way out is on foot to the west."

At least now Lowky knew something: *They were cut off, but how? Was it just the trucks and cars? The newsagents must have travelled to their shop somehow. Or maybe they'd never left!*

Lowky couldn't wait to get home. He picked up his pace, but as usual Dog was ahead, always waiting, always patient. It was when Lowky got through a particularly deep split that he noticed Dog digging at a piece of debris. He was sniffing frantically and circling it with his nose.

"Find some food, did you, Dog?" Lowky said as he sat down. He was tired but didn't want to deprive Dog of his treasure. Billy was frantic though, and within a minute Lowky was up again.

"What is it, Dog? Hey, boy, what is it?" Lowky started to move the broken bricks when he heard a small cry, *a cat maybe,* he thought. The more he moved the louder the cry became. Finally he moved a small piece of wood, which opened up into a collapsed room. Right at the top of the gap was the head and shoulders of a small boy, about 5 years old. The rest of the boy was cocooned by pieces of wood that had once been part of the wall frame. His hair was blond and matted in large clumps around his face. His blue eyes were swollen from crying.

"Oh, mate, are you all right?" Lowky choked as he struggled to move more of the debris. "Are you hurt?" Lowky asked frantically, which made the boy cry even more. "What's your name?" Lowky persisted, more calmly this time.

"Sam," the boy sobbed, looking woefully into Lowky's eyes.

"Okay, Sam, it's okay." Lowky kept coaxing as he continued to move the wood and brick from around his head and shoulders. Lowky made a big enough gap and then grabbed Sam by the armpits.

Sam screamed, "Leg, stuck!" and Lowky stopped immediately.

"Okay, Sam, I'm going to try again more slowly; you try and wiggle your leg out, okay?"

Sam nodded and Lowky whispered, "Ready, Sam? One ... two ... three!" He pulled slowly, but Sam would not budge.

Lowky stroked the boy's hair while he tried to think of something. Instinctively, Billy started to move. He squeezed through the gap Lowky had made near Sam's shoulders. That part of the building was kind of standing, and Lowky could see a small gap near Sam's legs and feet.

Billy turned around and came back out again.

"Okay, Sam," he said, "I'm going to move some more of this stuff from around your head and see if I can come in and free your legs. Okay?"

Sam was crying so hard at this point that all he could do was blink.

Lowky worked fast. He made sure his footing was right from the beginning, and within a couple of minutes he had cleared a rather wide space. The only thing stopping him was two wooden beams about half a metre apart, but he thought he could squeeze Sam through.

"Okay," Lowky said gently. "I'm going to wriggle in and free your leg. Then I'm going to come and pull you out. You're very brave." Lowky smiled but couldn't look at Sam. It had to be done whether Sam liked it or not, so he got on his stomach and wiggled his body halfway in. There was about half a metre of room around him, but not enough to get in properly.

Sam had been saved by a clearing about half a metre high, one metre wide, and one metre deep. His right leg seemed unharmed, but his left leg was stuck under some twisted wood and rubble.

Lowky started to lift the concrete from Sam's leg and placed it in the space to his left. He moved the last bit of wood and screamed back to Sam, "Try and move your leg!"

He could see the boy's leg moving as Lowky started to wiggle back out. Again he grabbed Sam under his armpits and slowly pulled.

Sam was crying again, but when he got out he hugged Lowky so tight that Lowky had to pry him off to check the boy's injuries.

Sam had a pretty bad cut that under normal circumstances would have required stiches, but nothing was broken, and with a bit of smooth talking, he finally started to settle down.

Having a small injured boy to travel home with certainly made Lowky's life more interesting, especially when he had to give him a piggyback ride.

CHAPTER 7

Possums

NOTHING had changed at home. The smell was getting better with the last of the rotting food finally turning to dust. Lowky carried Sam to the bed of coats, where he fell asleep almost immediately.

Once Lowky started a fire, he decided to spend some time in the kitchen. He looked more carefully for any last salvageable supplies. He struggled to get to the cupboards under the sink but managed to find:

> 4 saucepans
> 1 plate
> 2 cups
> 1 plastic glass
> 3 plastic containers
> 1 lunch box
> 2 drink bottles
> 1 jug

Lowky was hungry, and before making another trip to the kitchen he decided to make dinner. He looked at the neat piles of food all in rows and categories. He had sweet and savoury in separate sections; these were then divided into rows of cans, jars, cartons, and packets. He put together what seemed to be the easiest meal: one packet of pasta and one jar of sauce.

"Not bad," he said to Billy when they finished. He had never made pasta before, but he had eaten plenty of it. The dog and the boy ate gratefully as they sat gazing into the fire.

Billy was tired and curled up to go to sleep, but Lowky stayed awake. He decided to make one last trip to the kitchen.

It wasn't long before Lowky had unloaded his treasures. Now he only had the pantry left to check, and he knew it was almost empty because that was where he had collected his first lot of supplies. He decided to finish it off before morning. After all, he was wide awake and no one was going to tell him to go to bed.

He was just about to open the pantry door when he thought he heard a noise. He stopped. He hadn't seen any rodents but imagined some had survived. Maybe it was a rat? He wasn't scared of them, but he didn't really want one scurrying out at him. Maybe it was a possum? He wasn't scared of those either, but he *definitely* didn't want one of those coming at him.

Bang! He heard the sound of a falling can. The fright made him jump and almost fall on a stray piece of wood. He was petrified. He sneaked as quietly as a mouse back into the lounge room.

Dog was now standing, on guard in the doorway. Lowky grabbed him, and they both hid behind the tilted door. *Don't be ridiculous, Lowky*, he thought, *toughen up, for crying out loud, all this over a possum.*

"That's it, Dog," he said. "We're going to the pantry."

Dog was ready for action.

They walked with purpose to the pantry door. With one big combined breath, Lowky turned the handle. Instantly the room turned to anarchy. Flour, broken jars, and cans came flying out.

There was screaming, and a flour-covered creature came hurling towards them.

"Run, Dog, run!" Lowky screamed as he headed towards the door.

They both leaped over the fire as they grabbed a screaming Sam. Lowky snatched a piece of burning wood to use as a weapon. It worked; the flour monster stopped in the doorway and started to laugh. In fact, it laughed so hard it almost fell over.

"Wait a minute," Lowky panted. "Matilda?"

"Yes, Lowky, you big idiot," she squealed as she ran around the fire to hug him. Then she cried. He didn't have to ask why.

"You hungry?" he asked soothingly. "I've managed to collect quite a few things."

"I've noticed." She laughed with a smile as broad and warm as her heart. "What you got?"

"Some leftover pasta." He smiled.

"Anything to drink?"

"Water."

"Who's the boy?" Matilda asked. "And the dog?"

"Long story," Lowky replied. "You should eat first." He paused. "God, it's good to see you."

Matilda drank and ate with great gusto. It had now been six days since the earthquake, and this was the first time she'd had any decent food. Her house had collapsed except for two and a half rooms, but unlike Lowky's house her kitchen was not left standing. Luckily Matilda had just been to the Melbourne Show. She had bragged about how she had been saving all year. Then she bragged even more when she came home with eighteen show bags. She had been living off the lollies, chips, and drinks in them till now. Eventually, when her supplies ran out, she decided to try and find her mother. Matilda had not wanted to leave the house in case someone came home. Like Lowky, she had heard noise in the street, so she knew there must be a way of getting around. After four days, she went looking for her mum, who worked in a childcare centre just north of the house. It had been engulfed by the major split and nothing had survived. Matilda didn't know that at the time, though, so she'd tried. The devastation was so immense that it took all day. She didn't care if anyone saw her then; she could have used the help. It wasn't until she stood on a high pile of rubble that she saw the split ahead. It was so huge that she couldn't see the other side. It was so deep that she couldn't see the bottom. It was then that she knew her mother was dead.

"What about your uncle Richard?" Lowky asked.

"Lowky, if you had seen the split, you'd understand."

It was when Matilda finally got back to Overhill Road that she decided to look for Lowky or at least some food.

While Matilda ate, Lowky filled her in on everything that had happened.

*

The next morning, while Lowky was feeding everyone, Matilda prepared to go back to her house. Lowky automatically went into leader mode as Sam had a tantrum over the cereal. As usual Billy ate his food eagerly and gratefully and then waited at the door.

"Not today, Dog," Lowky whispered. "Tomorrow, okay? Rest today, you'll need your energy."

Billy plonked down but refused to move from the door.

"Suit yourself," Lowky said as he started to make a pile of all the bags and backpacks he could find. Just as he was about to make a pile of jackets, Matilda walked towards him, smiling.

"I'll see you soon."

"Are you sure you don't want me to come?" Lowky asked.

"No way, you stay here, there's a heap to do. I'll be fine." She turned and headed towards the door.

"Come on, Billy," she said soothingly.

Billy immediately got up and led the way.

"Traitor," Lowky said with a laugh. He had managed to get into one of the drawers under the couch, which contained smaller camping items. He also got into the coffee table drawer, which had split in two. He manoeuvred his wrist and scooped out some very interesting items.

By the time Matilda got back, Lowky had piles everywhere: one of food, clothes, jackets, bags, first aid, water, and one Lowky liked to call Extreme Scouts. In this pile is where he put all the curious items

> 3 elastic bands
> 1 strip of bag ties
> 1 bag of very thin pieces of rope
> 2 leather belts
> A ball of string
> Wrapping paper

3 canvas shopping bags

3 notepads

2 pens

A screwdriver

1 torch

1 very small tarp (1 metre squared)

1 fuel bottle

The toastie iron

1 camping stove

1 bag of tent pegs

1 silver hypothermia blanket

The last item made Lowky laugh. It looked like one huge piece of tin foil, and maybe on this trip it would serve both purposes.

Without saying a word, Matilda walked into the room carrying four bags. She had three backpacks, one on her back and one in each hand. Slung across her shoulder was a satchel. Lowky grabbed the two bags from her hands and waited as Matilda took off the other pack and opened it onto the floor. She pulled out a much larger tarp, which she put in the "scouts" pile. Then she pulled out two towels and two toothbrushes. Lowky was ecstatic. He hadn't brushed his teeth since before the quake and his mouth felt like a sandpit. Finally she pulled out some toothpaste, some pencils, and her sketchbook. She also put the pencils and book in the scouts pile and made a new pile for the toiletries. In the meantime, Lowky had opened the other two bags and started to hand each individual item to Matilda.

1 packet sherbet

1 bag of snake lollies

2 packets of chewing gum

A pencil case

2 thin blankets

1 comb

That was all that was in the bag, so he put it in the pile with all the others and moved on to the next one. He started with the pockets:

> 4 hair ties
> 1 note pad
> 1 jumper
> 2 hoodies
> 1 track suit pants
> 3 T-shirts
> 2 undies
> 2 pairs of socks

Lowky made a mental note to find some socks and undies. He had jackets and jumpers from the coat stand, but apart from that he had been wearing the same clothes. When he found the water tank, he had washed himself and the necessities, but he was sure he was starting to smell. He looked down at Sam whose ripped clothes were black with filth.

The only thing left was the satchel Matilda was still wearing. She slung it off her shoulder and slipped it between her legs. She looked different. Her long dark ponytail was darker and her face thinner than he had remembered. She took off a huge jacket that must have been her dad's and put it in the pile with the others. Out of the satchel she pulled a pillow.

"I can't sleep without it!" she said with a smile.

That was it! The combination of two lives on the floor. He looked around the room. It was way too much to carry, and they would have to make some very hard decisions.

Lowky pulled out a small backpack. "This one can be for Sam," he suggested.

"Okay! I'll take two—one on my front and one on my back," Matilda said as she grabbed the two most suitable packs. There was only one pack left, so Lowky took that, the satchel, and one of the canvas shopping bags.

"How shall we organise this?" he asked.

"Well, we need at least one bag of food and one bag of water." She paused. "We'll also need one bag for all our clothes, towels, and blankets . . ."

"We can use our jackets for towels and blankets; there's no point doubling up. We'll need a bag for camping gear," Lowky said.

"And one for Billy," she added.

"Okay, for the clothes, if we take one pair each and what we're wearing."

"One to wear and one to wash." Matilda agreed.

"Between the three of us, that will fill one bag." Lowky paused and then finished with, "And one jacket each. We can hang it over our packs while we're walking."

Things continued on like this for quite a while. Even the dog managed to look busy. In the end they agreed on almost everything except six items. They could carry only two.

Matilda's sketchbook and pencil case
The toastie iron
Billy's blanket
Little tarp
1 plastic plate, glass, and 2 plastic mugs
3 cans of baked beans

Matilda was insistent. "Why do we need the cups and plate? We've got the forks, so we can just eat straight out of the saucepan, and we've got six plastic water bottles. It's just a waste of space." She didn't bother to breathe. "And the tasty thingy, why do we need that? There's nothing to put in it anyway!"

"Well there would be," Lowky huffed, "if you'd let me take the baked beans!"

"I don't care what you take, but I'm taking my book and pencils."

"Matilda, really," he said calmly, "those beans could give us all two meals. Things have changed, and it really has to come down to necessity. Those beans could save our lives."

"I'm taking my book and *two* pencils, okay?" she snapped. "That gives you room for one of your stinky cans of beans."

"Matilda." Lowky was trying not to giggle; he had never seen her like this. He started to turn away, but she sensed it.

"It's not funny, Lowky, I've lost everything, and now you expect me not to draw. I have to draw! I have to!" At this point most people would have started crying, but not Matilda.

Lowky looked up at her just as she was starting to smile. "I'm taking my book!"

Matilda was right, she was always drawing. She didn't go anywhere without her black sketchbook, edition 9. She was given edition 1 as a present for her fifth birthday. It was hard-covered, and the paper was thick and crisp and white. It was of such good quality that Matilda said the *drawings drew themselves*. Matilda had been so impressed that she had refused to use any other book ever since. It had to be the same design and the same brand every time. She was just as meticulous with her drawing, taking weeks, months—and in one case—years to complete. She would often have five or six drawings on the go at one time, drawing them in layers and only when she could feel the mood of the drawing.

Lowky didn't really understand it, but he knew Matilda had to have her book. She had to draw!

"Okay, okay, take the book and two pencils." He caved.

"I was going to." She beamed.

"Well, that leaves room for one more thing," Lowky whispered. Instinctively he was most torn between the toastie iron and Billy's blanket.

When he told Matilda this she said, "No! It has to be the tarp."

It looked like Billy rolled his eyes and Matilda rolled around in the rubble laughing. "Why don't you take Billy's blanket and use some of the rope to tie your tasty thing to your pack?"

Lowky was frustrated and walked to the window to calm down. He looked at the old broken sill.

"Oh I can't forget these," he whispered, bending to search through the dirt on the floor. He picked up a crystal. His mum had given him a malachite crystal when he was born and then a crystal on his birthday every year after that. He had eleven. He never left the house without his malachite and on momentous occasions he took them all. It just so happened that on the day of the earthquake, Lowky had laid them carefully out on the windowsill to cleanse in the moonlight. He had laid them out in the order he had received them. He was planning to take them with him to his maths test the following day. He needed all the help he could get. Of course the first one he rescued from the floor was his malachite.

And that was it, everything was found, settled, packed, and attached. Tomorrow in the predawn they would leave for Spargo Creek.

CHAPTER 8

Protection

THERE was no alarm, no watch, no clock. It was still dark outside but it didn't feel like night time. Lowky listened for birds. There was nothing. The fire still had embers from the night before, so he added kindling and put some water on to boil. He did one final check of the bags and stashed all the remaining food. He found the perfect place under a big piece of slanted cement. Finally he made a big bowl of cereal and tried to eat it without waking anyone. It was impossible, and before long everyone was up and waiting for their turn with the saucepan. Lowky had already made three camomile teas, and they were now cool enough to drink.

While Lowky cleaned up, Matilda washed Sam and dressed him in some clean clothes. She had made another trip back to her house with Billy and had found a second pair of clothes for Lowky and some undies and socks for both boys. By this time, Lowky had finished washing the saucepan, two forks, one spoon, and Billy's bowl. He squeezed them all into his Coles bag and looked around at what was left of his house. He took a deep breath.

Matilda came and put her arm around his shoulder. "Don't worry, Lowky, we'll be back." She paused. "One day." With that, she grabbed her front pack and carried it out the door. She had cried yesterday when she'd said goodbye to her own house.

Lowky grabbed Sam's hand and smiled as he tried to get him to follow. "Come on, Sam, follow Billy. Were going to find a place to live." Lowky hesitated. "You've got the big, important pack with all the clothes in it, and we really need your help."

This worked, and Sam stood up a little straighter. "Thanks, Lowky," he said as he headed out to be with Matilda.

As always, Billy waited patiently for Lowky. He would not leave without him. "Okay, Dog," Lowky said as he took another deep breath. "Let's go."

Gee! What a funny looking bunch they were. All packed to the brim, hopeful but already tired. Lowky couldn't help staring at them all standing in the yard of rubble. Big jackets covering their goods, like humps. They looked like a tribe of wandering gypsies, and Lowky had to laugh out loud.

"What is it?" Matilda smiled.

"Let's go, Ms. Maya, this could even be fun." He giggled, ignoring her question.

"Okay, Mr. Tick, ready when you are," she mused.

"Hey, Sam, what's your last name?" Lowky asked with a nudge.

"Iffin, Sam Iffin."

"Did he say Fin?" he asked Matilda curiously, but she just shrugged. "Well, okay, little Fin, are you ready?"

"Weady." Sam stood behind Matilda as they ventured through the rubble, over the back fence, and into the lane. They headed back to the corner store. Lowky was carrying all the empty bottles and they stopped at the water tank to fill them. He had the knack of it now, so it didn't take long. Lowky moaned under the weight of the satchel. The water was now a thick brown colour and had been looking more putrid with every new batch.

"We shouldn't drink this till its boiled," he said.

Matilda agreed and they decided to wait until lunchtime to boil the water. Lowky was worried about their supplies and was happy to stretch things out. *How long do supplies last anyway . . . ?* Lowky thought. *How long will a bottle of water last? What about five bottles? How many a day? And how many days' walk to Spargo Creek?* Lowky thought intensely. In fact, he was so deep in thought that he got quite a shock when Sam interrupted him.

"I need a dwink, Lowky." He hesitated. "Pease!"

"We need to boil the water, Sam, to make it clean," Lowky reasoned.

"But I need some warer. I weally do! Pease!" Sam insisted as his eyes started to well up with tears. They were only at the end of the lane and they had all had a good drink before they left the house. Poor Sam! What was hard for Lowky must have been near impossible for Sam.

"Wait!" he shouted towards Matilda as he took his pack off and placed it neatly on the ruins near his green bag and satchel. "I'll just be a minute."

Matilda looked at him inquisitively.

"Sam, wait with Matilda and I'll get you a drink," he said proudly.

"Fanks, Lowy." Sam smiled.

Lowky had remembered the can of lemonade he had hidden back at the house; he took a big run up and jumped back over the split that divided the lane. He was happy for the distraction. It was a win-win situation. He was back at the house before he knew it. He was so wrapped up in his mission he had forgotten how difficult the terrain was. He went over to the beautifully hidden stash and grabbed the can of lemonade that was sitting perfectly in the front. He didn't have a bag and he needed both his hands to get back up the lane. He was sure that somewhere he had seen a small plastic bottle. He wondered what else they would need by the end of their journey.

He went back to the stash, and after much shuffling about, he found the bottle and bags. He put the can and the bottle in the bag and tied it to his belt. Without thinking, he moved to the door and turned around to ensure the supply was still well hidden. It was then something really weird happened: Lowky started to cry. In fact, he cried so hard he slid down what remained of the door frame. He didn't know how long it lasted but suddenly that voice in his head gently said, *That's enough, Lowky. They're waiting*! With that, Lowky got up, whispered a mantra of goodbye to his mum and sister, Tushita, and turned away for the final time.

When Lowky got back to the group, he realised he had been gone for quite a while.

"Are you okay?" Matilda asked. She was insightful, and Lowky had learned to trust her intuition.

"Yeah." He smiled. "I'm okay. I just had to get a drink for Sam." He undid the bag on his belt and handed the can to him.

"Don't drink too much. It has to last till lunch," Lowky said as he watched Sam struggle with the can. He took it back and opened it for him; then he poured it into the bottle before handing it back.

Sam drank it gratefully. He went to pass it to Matilda but she didn't want any, so Lowky put it in the satchel and slipped the plastic bag in the little side pocket.

"Okay then, are we ready?" Matilda asked gently.

"Ready," Lowky said.

"Yes," Sam said.

They all looked at Billy and waited for a response, but nothing.

They laughed and turned towards the back of the corner store.

"Now, if you see a map, batteries, or a radio, grab them. Otherwise it's really unstable so get to Overhill Road as soon as possible." Lowky tried to duck through the gap, but his pack was too big and he had to take everything off again. "Patience, Lowky, patience," he muttered. He was exhausted and they hadn't even made it to Overhill Road yet. *How is this ever going to work?*

He scrambled through the store with his pack perched in front of him. He could barely move, little own help anyone else. He decided to drop his stuff on Overhill Road and go back in.

Lowky saw Matilda struggling with two packs and a frightened Sam. He smiled, which turned to laughter. It was contagious, and before long they were all on the counter laughing happily. They looked at Billy, but nothing!

"Come on, Sam, come with me," Lowky said as he grabbed Sam's hand and one of Matilda's packs and headed back outside. The sun was already much higher in the sky than they had planned. They had decided they would travel in the early morning and evening. It was the most they would be able to manage with Sam, and it was the safest. They thought they had enough food for one and a half weeks, but water was a problem. Lowky figured the bottles would only last three days, and that was without using it for washing.

"So which way?" Matilda asked. "You said Spargo Creek was north, but I went that way looking for my mum and there is a massive split. We can't cross it—it must be sixty metres wide."

Lowky found this hard to believe but let her finish.

"I'm serious. There's nothing that could cross that."

"Well, remember the newsagents I told you about?" he asked, waiting for Matilda to respond. "Well . . ." he continued impatiently. "I doubt they were staying there, so they must be staying elsewhere. They must have gotten in somehow!" he reasoned.

"Staying where, Lowky? Have a look around! Look at us!"

"I think they came from somewhere else," he said, ignoring her, "so that means there has to be a way out. Let's go down Birnt Street for now. There are heaps of shops, so maybe we can find water."

"Okay," she said dramatically as she headed for the intersection of Overhill and Birnt.

Lowky hadn't been on that side of Overhill Road yet and was surprised at how widespread the damage was. Whenever he reached a high vantage point, he looked around hopefully, but he just saw rubble and "halves": half buildings, half roads, half sheds, half cars, and half fences.

Birnt Street was a massive shopping strip that went for at least ten kilometres. It was much bigger than the Overhill Road shops. They had already passed a bank, money exchange, electrical store, 7-11, and a noodle shop, which were all recognisable but damaged beyond repair. He couldn't make out the other buildings; the destruction was immense. In front of them were the remains of a three-story office building that had collapsed onto the road. The debris was at least one-story high, and although the climb was daunting it would make for a good vantage point.

Lowky took Matilda's front pack and put it on so she could help Sam.

They finally got to the top, and the flattened view was devastating.

"Look! There!" Matilda pointed.

Lowky looked to the right and saw a thick dark line about five kilometres away. "What is it?" Lowky asked.

"That massive split in the earth I was telling you about," Matilda replied as she raised one single eyebrow.

They tried to follow the line further around to the right, only to find it went as far as the eye could see. As they followed it back to the left and then straight in front of them, it seemed there was a gap in the split where it became much thinner and even seemed to disappear.

"We'll have to go that way," Lowky said.

"It looks like we can take Birnt Street almost all the way," Matilda said as she took a sip of lemonade and handed it back.

It was almost another hour before they came across a partially standing IGA about halfway between them and the split.

"Stop here for food?" Sam pleaded. He had refrained from complaining almost all day.

"Okay," Lowky said, "it's a good spot. Maybe we can find some stuff in that IGA. It looks easy enough to get into."

"I'll go," Matilda said. "You get the fire started so we can boil this water."

"Okay." He turned to Sam. "Do you want to come with me, to make a fire?"

"No! Tilda," he insisted.

"No, Sam, you can't go in there; it's not safe. Stay with me, and we'll make the water clean."

"No! Tilda!" he said with a tantrum.

Lowky rolled his eyes and glanced at Matilda. She came towards them, smiling as usual, and bobbed down to Sam's level.

"Come on, sweetheart," she said. "I'm sorry, but you can't come with me, it's not safe, sweetheart, and I need someone who can make a fire." She smiled as she watched him straighten up.

"I can make fire, I show you."

"Okay, you do that and I'll get Billy some dog food, okay?"

"Okay," Sam said, satisfied.

"Oh, you're good," Lowky said. "Real good."

Lowky easily found wood. He used what was once a picket fence for his main supply and found a damaged billboard for kindling. By the time Matilda came back, they had already boiled three bottles of water.

"See, Tilda?" Sam beamed. "I made fire."

"It's perfect, Sam, thank you."

"So what was it like in there?" Lowky asked hopefully. "Did you find anything?"

"Yeah, what do we need again? There are two whole aisles we can get to. One is dog food and cleaning products, so I picked up these. I didn't go to the other aisle yet. Oh—there are two registers at the front with a good supply of chocolates and lollies," she added as she placed down four cans of dog food. "What's for lunch?" She smiled.

Lowky suggested he could make some bread and tomato soup. Matilda and Sam eagerly agreed. Lowky got organised as Matilda went back into the store. This time she took Sam, ensuring Lowky that it was safe. Amazingly, in just one trip she managed to get a bag of dry food for Billy, some batteries, two cans of tomato soup, and a book.

Matilda came out, ecstatic. "They had my books! You know the ones I like, exactly the same one, in the next aisle, with the stationary" she beamed.

"Oh, and where are you going to put it?" Lowky snapped. "We can barely carry the food."

"Well excuse me!" she snapped back. "There were three sizes and I only took one, so you should be happy. Anyway . . ." She paused for emphasis. "You don't have to worry, I'll carry it,"

"Yes, you will," Lowky mumbled as he opened one of the cans of tomato soup. He hadn't meant to attack, so he smiled softly at her and asked her how much soup she wanted.

"A whole can; I'm starving."

"You're not *starving*," Lowky said.

"Whatever! We'll have a can each—it will make room for my book," she teased.

"Is there any Alfoil in that there supermarket, young lady?" He smiled again.

"I'll have a look; you're certainly in the right area."

Matilda came back with some Alfoil, and Lowky immediately added the dough he had made. He wrapped it up and eagerly put it in the fire.

"Look what I found," she said as she placed a sponge on the ground. "Oh, and these were at the counter." She pulled out four Snickers bars. "You should really have a look. It's awesome! I don't think anyone's been back here." She was pumped as she handed out the chocolate bars. "I'll be getting some more of these," she sang as she tried to stuff the last one in her pocket.

"And where will you put them?" Lowky mumbled, trying not to get annoyed.

"You'll carry them, Lowky, because you love chocolate." Again she was right, and Lowky blushed as he took a big bite of the bar. They sat silently for a while, enjoying the salty-sweet chocolate, but its divine caramel stickiness made everyone thirsty. After everyone had a drink and some soup, they had already used one full bottle of water.

"Was there any bottled water in there?" Lowky asked.

"I'm not sure; I don't think so." She thought for a second and then added, "Oh, maybe at the back."

Lowky got up and prepared to go inside. Before the earthquake, the IGA had been a reasonably big supermarket. There was a large, mainly undamaged car park at the back. The front doors were at the left of the store, the undamaged part. They were broken but standing.

He stepped through the broken glass and entered the store. Considering the circumstances, it was a little surreal. A pile of baskets was strewn across the entrance, and he grabbed one. A bakery at the edge of the store housed scattered mouldy bread and escaped flour. Some pumpernickel bread and a few savoury gourmet biscuits had held up well. He put them in the basket.

At the end of the bakery were two half aisles. They looked like they contained cereal and biscuits but had collapsed into themselves and were impossible to infiltrate. Next to them there were two full aisles that had stayed basically standing. Some of the last aisle had collapsed at the end, and most of the contents of the shelves were on the floor but accessible.

As usual Matilda was right, and the first aisle had pet food, cleaning products, and electrical items. He thought back to his list. Matilda had gotten batteries, so all he needed was a radio. This was the perfect aisle. He looked for a radio but had no luck.

He moved on to the next aisle and grabbed three different types of treats for Billy. They were all in a row on the floor.

1 bag of Schmackos
1 bag of Roo-Chews
1 bag of Pig's Ears

He put them in his basket as he negotiated the corner. The next aisle contained stationary, cake, bread mixes, Tupperware, and toys. Nothing useful really, but he grabbed a stuffed bunny for Sam and a bread mix just in case. By the time he walked back to the counter, his basket was full.

"I'll fix you up next time." He laughed as he searched the displays for a radio. "You're out of radios." He laughed again as he squeezed his way back through the broken door.

Sam was delighted with his toy and from that moment on would not let it go. Most of the time it was annoying, but Lowky was glad because it settled him down, especially at night.

"And where are you going to put that, Lowky Tick?" Matilda mocked.

"You'll see!" He laughed as he looked at the already-overflowing bags in the car park.

Lowky's bread turned out all right, but he decided to make the one from the packet so they could have some for the journey. He added the water, and once it was in the fire, he rested in the shade.

Sam and Billy fell asleep while Lowky and Matilda sat speechless, staring into their own private worlds. By the time Lowky turned the bread twice, the sun was setting low in the sky and the earth was starting to cool down. He gave Billy a whole packet of Schmackos and put the pig's ears in the pack where the can of soup used to be.

Matilda also started to get organised and somehow managed to attach the spare book to her bag.

Lowky laughed out loud.

"Seriously, Lowky!" she snapped. "Do you know how hard it's going to be to get these?"

"Impossible!" he laughed. They all loaded up their items and responsibility and looked straight ahead.

"One second," he yelled as he ran back into the supermarket to get four more chocolate bars. He also went back to the stationary section and grabbed Matilda the smallest version of her black book and hid it in the back of his pants. The group had already started heading back down Birnt Street when he caught up with them.

"What did you get?" Matilda asked.

"Oh, nothing, just had one last look for batteries," he said.

The next stretch of road was easier to manoeuvre. They had boiled the water, so even though they had to be careful with the amount they regularly stopped for small drinks.

Sam was tired before he even started, and after an hour of solid complaining, he refused to go any further.

Lowky was flabbergasted and tried to reason, plead, and ultimately beg him to get up. "Come on, Sam, we have to walk till it gets dark, and we need to find water." He added, "You can be the treasure hunter and the treasure is water; if you find it you get a surprise." Lowky remembered the chocolate bars he'd slipped into his jacket.

Sam was reluctant to play along but managed to keep walking for a while before he started complaining again.

This time Lowky was relieved by the interruption. The silence was beginning to create a space of fear. He could think of nothing other than *why*? The more he thought, the more the water welled up in his eyes. His whole energy was being consumed by the desire not to cry.

His grief was overwhelming, but Sam's was worse! Sam couldn't hold back and was constantly asking for his mum.

Matilda smiled the most, but that had always been her way.

He looked at her now, her eyes swollen with silent crying.

"Let's stop," Lowky dramatically announced. "That's enough for the first day; were all tired. I'm done!" With that, he threw off his way-too-heavy pack and plonked himself on top of it.

Sam and Matilda stood there staring.

They were on the edge of what looked like a full block of demolished buildings. The ground was completely uneven, and even the exposed road was mainly destroyed. It was not the ideal place to set up camp, and the sun was still far from the horizon.

It seemed like they stayed like this for ages—the younger two staring at the defeated leader. All Lowky could do was hang his head and breathe deeply. He did this melodically, focusing only on his breath. Remembering how to breathe. Waiting for his breath to return to normal. Hoping his breath would heal. He was like a statue, heavy, concrete, unable to move. Lowky's head slouched as he looked at his belly button. His scraggly brown fringe fell into his eyes no matter how many times he flicked it away.

Finally the silence was broken by Matilda's soft laughter. She gently touched Lowky's shoulder. "Come on, we can't camp here." She kindly took his hand and pulled him to his feet.

He didn't say a word, but Matilda said one last thing before they all slipped back into their silence. "There is something still standing in the next block. Maybe we can camp there." She put her packs back on, took Sam's hand, and started to lead the two sulking boys over the rubble towards the setting sun.

CHAPTER 9

Malachite

Lowky walked towards the lonesome building with his head down most of the way. Matilda ignored this while she attended to Sam's many needs.

"Tilda, I need water. Tilda, I don't want to walk anymore. Tilda, I'm tired . . . I'm hungry . . . Tilda! Tilda! Tilda!"

Billy stayed with Lowky, walking slowly until finally they all stopped. One very large piece of fence was crumpled in their path. Matilda lifted Sam up and tried to place him on the other side, but the ground was split and the drop was more than a metre. Sam started screaming. She tried desperately to pull him back over, but his bag was hitched to the fence, and the more she tried the more Sam screamed.

"For crying out loud, Lowky, will you help here?" Matilda yelled.

Lowky moved slowly although he was trying to move fast. His body didn't care, and the faster he ran the slower his motion seemed. Finally he got to the fence. Billy started barking frantically at what they thought was the chaos and excitement of the situation.

"I'll jump the fence and grab him from the other side," Lowky said.

"Quick," Matilda said as she tried to shift her grip. "Lowky, quick, I'm losing him!"

Lowky tried at three points to get over the fence, every time falling back onto the side he had started from. Matilda and Sam were screaming at this point. Billy was still barking, but Lowky noticed that the sound was getting further away. He tried to turn around but was perched precariously on the fence. He was attempting to swing his leg over when the whole thing crumpled down another half metre from his weight.

It was all too much for Matilda, who dropped Sam without warning. Sam's screams became so loud it sounded like he was being tortured.

Matilda's hand was squashed between the newly crumpled sections of the fence, and it made it impossible for her to manoeuvre herself to the other side.

At this point, Lowky managed to cross over the fence but then realised Billy was still on the other side.

"Matilda, Billy!" he screamed. She turned around but couldn't see him. Sam was still screaming.

"Sam, stop!" Lowky yelled, but this just made it worse. "Sam, I need to listen for Billy, will you *stop*!"

Sam looked up at him, devastated, his bottom lip quivering, and for just a second he stopped crying.

"I can hear him," Matilda yelled. "He's back there somewhere. Get my hand out, Lowky, and I'll go and get him!"

Lowky was about five metres down the fence, and again it seemed like forever before he could get to her. As he approached, he realised there was only one chance and that was to pull her arm from underneath. He cringed as that would mean pulling it out of its socket. He froze for a second and looked her straight in the eye.

"Oh, geez," he mumbled as he started to pull at her arm. Matilda whacked him with her other hand.

"What are you doing, you idiot? You're going to pull my arm off."

Lowky stopped, shocked by the situation, and waited until Matilda spoke again. "My arm is just caught at the wrist. Is there any way you can loosen that bit of fence?"

Lowky estimated where Matilda's wrist was and tried to lift the fence.

"Go slowly," she whispered. "I don't want you to slice my wrist."

Lowky slowly pulled and tugged at the fence. He couldn't get his footing, which made it almost impossible to get into the right position. He took a deep breath and balanced on a piece of wall.

"Nearly . . . nearly, Lowky . . . careful!" she whispered as she slid her arm out. Miraculously, apart from a deep scratch, she was uninjured. She looked at the dripping blood and stoically said, "I'll fix this up once I've got Billy."

She looked for Billy, frantically listening for his barks. She could sense danger ahead and was too scared to call out. Billy sounded enraged and defensive and she scrambled over the rubble to help him. Matilda got to a fairly high vantage point, and she could see a crew of about seven SES workers in random pieces of orange clothing. She managed to laugh in the chaos of the situation. They looked like carrots in a white sauce.

Billy did not see the humour in the situation and was walking backward barking angrily as they tried to approach him.

"It's all right, boy," they said soothingly as they put their hands up in a sign of friendship. Billy just kept barking and retreating.

Matilda didn't know what to do. She didn't want to blow her cover but she couldn't lose Billy, either. She called out as quietly as she could: "Billy, come!"

Billy turned towards her, but so did the SES workers.

"Hey, sweetheart, you all right?" yelled the biggest, gruffest one.

"Come, Billy, run!" This time, Matilda screamed. In fact she screamed so loud Lowky was sure he heard something.

He had been trying to console Sam, who was uninjured but badly shaken. Sam refused to be consoled, and although he was not so panicked, he was still sobbing and refused to move. Lowky got back up and looked over the crumpled fence. But he couldn't see Matilda. Lowky thought he must be hearing things, so he went back to attending to Sam. Within a minute he heard shuffling and scratching and got back up to look over the fence again. He was horrified when he saw the way Billy was running towards him, but he was truly petrified when he saw Matilda's face.

"Grab Sam!" she yelled. "Run!"

Lowky had no idea what was going on but knew it was important, so he bundled Sam up and tried to scurry forward. This sent Sam into absolute hysteria, and even Lowky was surprised by the results. Sam started to kick and scream like a child possessed. When he finally broke free of Lowky he stamped on his foot and headed screaming towards the fence and Matilda. As this was all happening Billy jumped the fence and clipped his toe on the way over, and this made him yelp as he landed skewwhiff and summersaulted to an awkward stop. Matilda was still trying to climb over the fence when Lowky saw the crew of orange approaching.

"Run, Matilda! Run!" Lowky screamed as she too summersaulted to the ground. Her hand was now quite bloody from the cut and she left a red handprint as she got to her feet. Sam was pulling at her waist, still screaming, as she tried to move forward.

"We have to move forward, Sam, we have to run," Lowky insisted.

"I'll get Sam, Matilda, you go ahead, just grab the packs, and just run!"

Matilda ran frantically ahead, once she was out of sight she dropped all the bags and kept running. Billy stayed behind with Lowky.

Lowky looked at Sam for less than a second and then tried to pick him up again, but Sam was impossible. He screamed, he punched, he kicked. At one point he kicked Lowky right in the balls. Lowky dropped him and fell to his knees. Sam was shocked and just stood there staring, tears rolling down his face, mouth open, frozen.

"Sam," Lowky squeaked, "you don't understand. We can't stay here. They're going to catch us and then we'll be separated." At that very moment something really weird happened: he saw a flash of images, like *photos* before his eyes: a *photo* of Sam at one, at two, at three. In all these photos Sam was with a family, each family different, but he was never alone.

"Sam, do you want to stay here?" Lowky asked reluctantly. "The orange people will take you somewhere safe and might even find someone in your family." Lowky paused. "Sam, what do you want to do?"

Sam just cried, and Lowky knew that ultimately he had to make this decision. It was a decision that required much deliberation, much thought and consideration, and he had about two seconds to make it.

He immediately put his hand into his pocket, pulled out the chocolate bars, and fumbled around until he found the crystals his mum had given him. He swiftly handed the malachite to Sam and said, "This will protect you, I am always here for you; we are like brothers." He glanced at the approaching SES. "This crystal will protect you while we're apart. You need to try and find your family, and this is how you can do it. If you're not happy, meet me next year on your birthday. It's the forth of December, right?"

Sam nodded.

"Meet me on the corner of Overhill and Koves road. You'll be six then, but if you can't get there this time I'll go there ever year on that date at eleven a.m. until you can."

Sam nodded again, and Lowky felt like grabbing him while he was distracted. He hesitated. "You can always come back to us, Sam, if you need too."

Lowky quickly pulled his little book out of the back of his pants and wrote down the details. He tore out the paper and wrapped it around the crystal.

Sam smiled calmly as Lowky buried the parcel deep inside Sam's pocket and reminded him not to lose it. With that, he turned around and scrambled for his life.

Billy sensed the urgency and effortlessly bounded over the rubble. They ran until the noise of the SES drifted away; they ran till they could run no more. They looked at each other knowingly. The SES were obviously distracted by Sam, so they hide behind a partially standing building until the noise completely slipped away. He didn't look back—there was no point. His eyes were filled with tears, so he wouldn't have been able to make Sam out anyway.

CHAPTER 10

──◦──

Bean

"**O**H geez, Billy! How will we find Matilda? How will I tell her about Sam?" Lowky put his head in his hands and sighed dramatically.

Billy got up and continued walking up Birnt Street. Lowky followed. This was becoming the pattern.

"Shouldn't we go get the packs?" Lowky shouted in a shaky whisper. Billy just lifted his head and continued walking. Again Lowky followed. It made sense really; the partially standing building ahead was where Matilda should be. Lowky's thoughts were spinning so fast he started getting dizzy. Had he made the right decision? Could he have done things differently? Was he a bad person?

He tried to calm himself down. *It doesn't matter now,* he thought. *It's too late anyway!* But it didn't work—it made matters worse. The more he worried, the more he panicked. His hands started to sweat. His skin was cold and clammy. His breath was shallow. He tried to swallow, to swim to the surface, but his lungs were filling up with fear, and he was drowning in it. The more he panicked the more hopeless things became. The tears ran silently down his face. He felt so alone he didn't even bother to cry out loud. Then, without warning or request, he heard that inner voice again. Softly and peacefully it repeated: *All is well.*

Slowly, methodically, he started moving forward, taking steps towards Billy. Lowky was suddenly disturbed by a sound, and he immediately spun around. He was looking for Sam, but nothing was there. He was sure he could hear him, so he turned back and ran towards the fence and the sound, scraping his knees as he stumbled and fell.

Billy stayed where he was and waited. Before long, Lowky fell to the ground again, and this time he didn't bother getting up. He lay his head in the rubble and sobbed.

Billy did nothing. There was nothing he could do. He waited. And waited.

Finally Lowky got up and started walking again.

Billy moved slowly, unsure if he was being followed. He glimpsed Lowky quickly and saw him scraping his feet on the uneven surface. They walked like this for hours. Lowky refused to move any faster than an injured snail. Billy also felt the quiet and was happy to wait as Lowky endlessly caught up and then fell behind again.

All the time, *All is well* was playing in Lowky's head. He had stopped crying long ago and his heart and his head beat at a normal pace. Finally he lifted his head and looked at Billy, who was sitting on a platform waiting for him.

Lowky smiled and yelled hoarsely, "Wait up, Billy. Let's have some water."

Billy barked enthusiastically, and Lowky finally picked up his pace and started to hum "All Is Well, All Is Well."

The building in the distance had finally come clearly into view. It wasn't just partially standing as they had originally thought. It appeared to be fully standing. In fact, apart from some broken windows, it was as if the building had not received the "e-mail" about the earthquake, and was not aware that it was supposed to fall.

He could tell the building was a hardware store. He looked at Billy and then towards the horizon. Lowky joined Billy, who was already sitting comfortably and gazing at the sky. Although they were so close to the building and possibly Matilda, they sat there silently watching the sun turn a rainbow of yellows, oranges, and pinks. When the horizon had only a streak of yellow left and the sky was turning a deep blue, Lowky and Billy stood up and headed purposely towards the store, both a little lighter and happier than before.

About twenty metres from the store, Lowky started calling Matilda's name. It reminded him of the days after the earthquake when he had been searching for her. That seemed like a lifetime ago, and he marvelled at how much had happened and yet how close to home they still were. In fact, he could have travelled to this hardware store in twenty minutes on his bike on any other normal day.

Normal day, he thought with a giggle. Those days were far behind him. Billy barked.

"What is it, Dog?" he asked.

Billy was heading away from the shop and off to his left.

Lowky turned around and saw Matilda stick her head out from a mound of broken and twisted wood. Her beaming smile was contagious, and Lowky ran towards her unaware of the rubble he was passing over. He even managed to beat Billy to her, and when they finally got to each other they hugged and cried like long-lost relatives.

"Where's Sam?" Matilda asked almost immediately.

Lowky froze but Matilda smiled. He sat down where he stood and she followed. The stories that followed caused Matilda to stop smiling, and tears streaked her dirty face but finally she said, "It is what it is, Lowky. We can't control everything."

Matilda had run like a wild thing through the rubble when the SES had arrived. She didn't stop to think or breathe, and when she finally stopped she was at the building, a hardware store. She decided to hide until the others arrived. She had no supplies but didn't dare go back to the fence to retrieve the packs. She had no idea if Lowky had grabbed them. She was parched but held out little hope the hardware store would contain water or food. She decided to wait for reinforcements, so she found a pile of debris that looked like the remains of an old wooden sign. It created some shade and protection. Part of the shattered sign lay over the top of a ditch, so she would not be spotted from the land or sky. She sat there silently for hours before she started to really worry. She thought of all the possible escapes the boys might have attempted and even the most complex versions wouldn't have taken this long. She'd timidly poked her head above the mound and scanned the terrain. There was no sign of Lowky, Sam, or Billy. Matilda was beginning to get desperate. She could think of only two possible scenarios. Either they had been captured or they were hiding. Again Matilda decided to wait in her fortress, this time scanning the area for the approach of her friends. It wasn't until she checked at sunset that she saw the outline of something unfamiliar. It was too far away to make out for sure, and it seemed the object was stationary. Matilda dared not approach it so she again stayed hidden, checking regularly on the object. Finally, as darkness approached, so did the object. Matilda watched in anticipation, but by the time it was close enough to make out it was too dark to see. Seconds later, Matilda heard Lowky's voice calling her. As she lifted her head, Billy started to bark and she could finally make out his silhouette.

"What now?" Lowky asked, smiling genuinely.

"Well, we can try and find food and water in the hardware store, but it's already dark, and . . . I've heard banging coming from in there," she added tentatively.

"We could go back and get our packs," Lowky suggested. They both laughed nervously.

"Back to the fence, Lowky, really, in the dark?" she mused.

"Well, why not? At least we'll get some food and we can come back here before morning."

Matilda laughed even harder this time. "There and back in the dark."

"Yes." He smiled; usually he would have given in to a slump of hunger and self-pity. But he finally felt he was up for the adventure. "Let's do it, Matilda. Come on, it's a full moon." He hesitated for a second. "Think noodles, bread rolls, water—"

"Okay, okay, I'm in," she interrupted.

Billy instinctively got up.

"Grab Billy's collar," Matilda added, and with much giggling and fumbling they headed back down Birnt Street, towards home. Of course Billy was amazing, leading them graciously and patiently towards the fence.

He waited regularly for one of the fallen children to get back on their feet and reattach themselves to his collar.

The conditions for their late-night journey were excellent. The moon was bright and huge as it lifted off the horizon. The weather was clear and mild, and they were in good spirits. They were so caught up in the moment it wasn't until Billy refused to go any further that they realised they were already there.

With the help of the moonlight, it didn't take long to locate their packs. Lowky found the chocolate bars he had thrown out of his pockets and handed one to Matilda.

"Let's share one," she said practically. "I didn't see anything else standing between here and the split, and I doubt there's any food in a hardware store."

Lowky nodded and put the other two bars back in the pack. He immediately went looking for wood for the fire and found an easy supply.

In the meantime, Matilda found dog food and fed a very hungry Billy. Before long the fire was roaring and Billy had gone to sleep in Matilda's lap. Lowky had already heated up a can of beans and passed them to Matilda with a fork. She ate them, mindfully savouring every flavour: the salt, the tomatoes, the sugar. She leaned back against the rubble and thanked her lucky stars, and then she opened her eyes and named one. It was just below the Southern Cross and she called it *Bean*.

Lowky had always loved to cook, and his mum had given him much freedom in the kitchen and on the campfire. He effortlessly made some noodles and damper—his campfire bread surprisingly successful—and added some random spices for flavour. He was dying for some fresh food, anything—he would even eat zucchini gratefully. But all he had was dried herbs, and it seemed like a feast. The damper was much more successful than his attempt the night before, and dipped in the noodles and beans it was heaven.

Lowky served up a small plate for Billy, and they all sat engaged in their meals. When Matilda couldn't eat one more thing she started to laugh. She laughed hysterically; later she would describe it as an overdose of nutrients, but at the time there was no explanation. Lowky started to laugh as well, and before long they were all horizontal in the dirt. The moon covered them with a protective light, and the stars were more vibrant than they had ever been.

Lowky took out his remaining crystals to cleanse them in the moonlight.

Lowky and Matilda started to pack up. This happened seamlessly as they organised themselves. Billy slept, which surprised Lowky. He was usually a few metres ahead, anticipating the next move. Lowky was reluctant to wake him, and to his relief he woke, stretched, and proceeded back to the hardware store just seconds before them.

The supplies were back to full capacity, and Lowky and Matilda had to share Sam's bag. This made the journey slower, but with their full bellies (and spirits), it didn't really matter.

Two days of travelling had left them battered and bruised, and by the time they got back to the hardware fortress, they were exhausted. They were too tired to attempt the hardware store, so they pulled out their jumpers and made their beds in the smoothest patch they could find. Billy curled up with Lowky to share his warmth.

They slept soundly that night, and when they woke at first light, they were ready for anything—and they would need to be!

CHAPTER 11

——◯——

Maniacs

MATILDA had already started a fire and put a pot of water on as Billy and Lowky woke up. They both stretched simultaneously and sat by the fire.

"So what's the plan this time, Einstein?" Lowky teased.

"Easy!" Matilda retorted. "We go and get supplies. We'll need ropes and batteries, and I'm sure we can get a radio. I'm dying to hear news, Lowky, any news, news of anything, even news that there's no news is news at least."

She lost him there, and he started to chew on some of the damper from the night before.

"It would also be nice to sleep somewhere comfortable."

"We can't sleep here," Lowky snapped. "We need food, Matilda, and fresh water, and we need to get to Spargo Creek. We need to keep moving."

"Yeah, I get it! But we need to be able to move, Lowky, and look at your legs."

Lowky looked down and examined his injuries in detail. His knees had been shredded on his many trips and falls. He had two huge gashes, one in his thigh and one in his forearm from the tin fence where they'd lost Sam. His ankle was swollen and he had blisters on both his heels from his dirty sneakers.

"We need to stock up and rest or we won't make it anywhere. Let's just see what we can find." Matilda spoke steadily, but Lowky knew she was upset.

He smiled an apology and headed towards the store. He hadn't heard any noises and was convinced it was empty. Whether it was untouched or not was anyone's guess.

The front entrance had a steel security door that must have rolled down in the shaking. The display windows on either side of the door were shattered, so they decided to enter that way. He grabbed the window frame carefully and pulled himself inside. Just as he entered, a shard of glass came crashing down from the top of the window frame, missing him by only centimetres. As a result, a small scratch appeared, and Lowky felt it bleeding as he lifted Billy over the glass. The store wasn't your big-scale hardware like Bunnings Warehouse; it was a family store that looked as if it had been standing for hundreds of years. It had an old and dusty feel that seemed to outlive the chaos of the earthquake.

Lowky stepped off the display platform and looked around as Matilda crawled in. They were both standing there, quite amazed at the cleanliness and order of the place when all hell broke loose.

There was an aisle directly in front of them with shelves on either side. Out of both sides came two wrench-bearing maniacs. They were screaming uncontrollably as they raced around too fast to be identified. They did a final squeal as they ducked back into the rows of shelves.

Matilda and Lowky were stunned. They could hear whispering behind the shelves as they ducked for cover into the displays on their right. Before they had a chance to hide themselves, the screaming maniacs where running around again, this time throwing hammers and screwdrivers at them. Every time Matilda and Lowky would try and duck for cover, they would cut them off, waving their arms and chanting like crazed lunatics. All the while Billy barked and snapped, but all he got was large mouthfuls of air. Finally they managed to scramble back through the broken window and into the safety outside.

No more noise was heard from the store, and after a couple of hours they felt comfortable to stoke up the fire and have something to eat. After a lot of deliberation they decided they would approach the store again after lunch. This time they would need a plan. Matilda pulled out her little black book and started writing some notes. She wrote:

- The maniacs were small and appeared to be children.
- They were armed and dangerous.
- They were strong.
- They had completely lost their minds.

Matilda read the list to Lowky to see if he had anything to add.

"No, that's very comprehensive," he muttered. "Why don't we try going around the back next time?" he added as he grabbed the book from Matilda's hands.

"And how would we get there? There's no access! No, we should go through the front. At least we know the layout." She added, "Hey, let's throw in a note!"

"Saying what?'

"Declaring peace and explaining that we can't move on until we've rested. Maybe they're on their own?"

"I doubt it," Lowky said. "Maybe we should just move on. Surely more buildings are standing on the other side of the split."

"You said it yourself, Lowky—we can't move on until we at least fill up our bottles with water." She paused. "Without Sam, we still have enough food for three days if we only eat once a day."

"We could make bread to last us five days," he added.

"But the bottom line is we need water and can't risk going on without it."

Lowky took a small swig of water from the last bottle and passed it to Matilda. She poured a little into Billy's bowl and then took a small sip herself. As Lowky capped the bottle, he imagined drinking its entire cold, wet contents. His mouth watered. He again opened his book and started penning a note with Matilda.

"Dear maniacs," Matilda started affectionately.

Lowky laughed and wrote, *Dear friends, we are children and we are on our way to a new home. We need water and shelter. Please let us know if you can help.* Lowky finished writing and looked up at Matilda.

"That's nice," she reassured him. "Now end with something sweet."

We intend only peace; we are two children and a dog, thank you. Lowky put the pen in his pocket as he finished the note.

"Oh, I don't know about the end, we need a good ending." Matilda was serious and Lowky couldn't help but laugh.

"What would you like me to write?" he asked.

"Our names!" Matilda teased.

Lowky looked at her kindly and then wrote, *Matilda and Lowky.*

Matilda smiled as she turned to put the pot back on the fire. Lowky quickly folded the paper into four pieces. He looked around to find a good-sized chunk of cement and hoped the maniacs would notice it as it whirled past their heads. He tied the note to the chunk with a red sock and handed it to Matilda for delivery. Matilda had always been a pro at sports, and compared to Lowky, well, there was no comparison. Matilda was a gun; Lowky was not.

Matilda held the sock-wrapped parcel in her left hand. She was right-handed except when it came to throwing things. Her palms started to sweat as she approached the door. After the last attack she knew anything was possible, and she approached with caution. Once inside she would have to draw attention to herself so the maniacs knew she was throwing something.

She sneaked in the window, but in less than a second the maniacs were hurtling and screeching towards her. She threw the rock at their feet, missing the loudest one by only millimetres. They momentarily stopped as if stunned by the flash of red. Matilda turned around and scampered out, her hands over her head for protection. The maniacs had never chased them outside, and by the time she was back at the campsite their cries where faint and harmless.

Matilda was full of adrenalin and she ran around the tiny space, high-fiving the air and whooping to herself. Lowky laughed, and then they sat and waited for a response. They didn't have to wait long. Within ten minutes the red sock came hurtling back out the window. Attached was a new note. It simply said, *Show yourself.*

Something about this made Lowky laugh; he felt like he was in a war zone and on the losing side. He had had enough. He just wanted a little peace. Without negotiation he strolled to the top of the mound. He stood defiant and exposed with his hands on his hips. Nothing happened.

Billy followed and sat beside Lowky. Still nothing.

Matilda didn't need to be asked; she scrambled onto the mound and smiled towards the store. They stood there for a minute or so and were just about to turn around and go back when a new rock came flying out; this one was tied in a black and blue striped sock. Matilda grabbed it and unfolded the note. It read, *Come inside—and bring my sock.*

Matilda stuffed the sock into her pocket and went to the food pack. She pulled out a chocolate bar to use as a peace offering. She stuffed it into the back of her pants as she only intended to offer it if absolutely necessary.

"Don't you think it's suspicious, them inviting us in after all that fuss?" Lowky said.

"Who knows what they've been through, Lowky?" Matilda said quietly. "They're just protecting their own. You'd do the same."

"Would I?" he muttered.

"Stop it, Lowky," she snapped. "There's no time to go on a guilt trip— Sam was not your fault. Now, we have a farm to find and vegetables to eat!" With that, she dusted off her T-shirt and started limping towards the store.

Billy waited impatiently for Lowky, and one by one they entered through the window display, un-attacked.

CHAPTER 12

Twins

Lowky and Matilda nervously faced the two maniacs: a boy and a girl. The girl stood closest. Her skin was tanned dark by the sun or culture. Her hair was distracting in its crazy dance away from her head. It was wild, curly wild! Her curls were dark and loose like a relaxed afro. It sat uneasily at her shoulders and highlighted her dark, intense eyes.

Matilda was right, Lowky thought. *They even look like maniacs.*

"My name is Lowky," he said.

She was shorter than him, but her face was wise so it was hard to tell her age.

"This is Matilda," Lowky added, pointing towards an unusually timid Matilda, "and Billy—Billy Baxter."

The girl looked at Lowky and then at the dog, and she smiled. Standing to her left was a similar-looking boy. He stood more staunchly in an attempt to look frightening. In a military-like fashion, his arms hung rigidly by his side. He looked a lot like the girl, and Lowky assumed they were brother and sister.

"I'm Marley," the girl said, still smiling at the dog, "and this is my twin brother, Chilli."

Chilli looked coldly at them. "What's your story?" he snarled. "Why are you here?"

"We've lost our family and our homes, but we know a place where we can live and are making our way there. We're in need of water, and that's why we entered your store." Lowky waited but there was only silence.

He could see Marley thinking. Chilli stood a little crouched just behind her. It looked as if he was waiting for Marley's reply even though he'd asked the question.

Finally Marley spoke. "We lost our dad. We don't know if he's alive."

"We're waiting for him," Chilli interrupted. "He's trying to get here. He won't be long."

"My mum and sister died, I don't really know what happened." Lowky paused for a second. "I think it was an earthquake?"

Chilli couldn't help but burst out laughing.

Lowky and Matilda learned Chilli and Marley had been much better off than them since the earthquake. They had ample food. Like a Hobbit hole, the Sal-Henco house had had numerous pantries and cellars. Mrs. Sal-Henco had loved to cook and had kept a well-stocked pantry. But it was Mr. Sal-Henco who had really thrived in the kitchen. He made pickles, chutneys, mustards, and jams. Anyone who tasted them wanted more. He made various eccentric combinations that could not be found in stores. They loved his cucumber and kiwi jam or his watermelon-stuffed olives. Marley's favourite was sweet pumpkin croutons, with mango and Persian feta, which he made often for her. Mr. Sal-Henco would never sell his concoctions and rarely made the same combination twice (his family's favourites were the exception). Instead, he would bake, pickle, and churn all year long, and like a modern-day Santa Claus on Christmas Day, every person he knew (and some he didn't) waited enthusiastically for their presents. It didn't matter what they got; no one was ever disappointed. That was until last year, when Mrs. Sal-Henco died. She had been sick for a long time, and her death turned Mr. Sal-Henco into a reclusive, anxious, and overprotective parent. This overprotection had a huge impact on Chilli, who uncharacteristically became "Daddy's little boy."

Marley looked supportively at her brother. "Wait here," she said as they slipped between the long rows of shelves.

Lowky heard them whispering but couldn't make out what they were saying. He looked at Matilda, who was searching the nearby items to see if there was anything they could use. Billy was at Lowky's feet, looking around, and ready to explore.

"No, stay here, Billy," Lowky whispered just as Marley and Chilli came back out.

Matilda froze and looked innocently at Chilli, who surprisingly was smiling.

Marley spoke first. "Sorry for the rude introduction," she said. "We've been hiding, and naturally we've become very protective." Her voice was relaxed and friendly and her face softened as she spoke. "It's been two weeks, and we've been completely hidden." She looked at Chilli and continued. "Come in and take a look; we have plenty of water and you can stay for dinner." She paused again but Lowky could tell she wasn't finished. "You can stay till morning, but then you have to leave." She glanced at Matilda. "If you're okay with that, then really it would be our pleasure. We could use the company."

Lowky and Matilda looked at each other and nodded knowingly.

"I'll go get our bags," Matilda announced as she headed back towards the broken window.

"Thank you," Lowky added as he turned to follow her. Billy jumped through the window in front of him and watched as Lowky struggled back to where they had stashed the packs.

Once they were out of earshot Matilda said, "They seem okay." She smiled cautiously. "I mean, I think they were just scared at first, don't you?" She didn't wait for a response from Lowky and continued. "I'm sure I would have acted the same." She took a deep breath and continued again. "How old do you think they are? They said dinner—maybe they have real food? Do you think it's safe? What if—"

"Yes, yes, and yes," Lowky said with a laugh. "No point worrying. I'd do almost anything right now for something different to eat, so let's go." He effortlessly threw his pack over his back and picked up the other packages as he turned to follow Billy back over the rubble. He felt rejuvenated, and so did Matilda. He turned around to flash her a smile. Even Billy was smiling.

When they returned through the window the twins were nowhere to be seen.

Lowky yelled out tentatively. "Marley . . . Chilli?"

"We're out back at the end of the shelves," they called in unison.

Matilda had lost all timidity and immediately headed down the closest aisle. Lowky and Billy followed.

When Matilda emerged at the other end, she suddenly stopped, and Lowky almost bumped into her.

"Oh gee," he whispered as he looked around the open space. It must have been a café at one point but all the chairs and tables had been moved except one. In the middle of the opening was a small but effective fire.

Lowky smelled bread cooking, and although he hated to admit it, it smelled much better than his. He also knew well the smell of coffee, and even though he had never tried it, he was willing, at this point, to try anything. In addition to the overwhelming and delightful smells, Lowky's eyes were almost popping out of his head. There was a small pyramid of jars towering over the counter behind the fire. On top of the counter was a ten-litre container of clear, clean water. Lowky's mouth watered as he tried to hold himself back. He reached into his own pack remembering that they now didn't have to ration their own water. His was brown and smelt like sewerage. Just as he was about to put it to his lips, Chilli came out from behind the pyramid with two large aluminium glasses.

"Hey, drink this." Chilli laughed reluctantly as he handed them the drinks.

Marley followed Chilli with a big bowl of water for Billy. They all drank happily. Lowky squatted down next to Billy, pulled out his bowl, and fed him the last of a very smelly can of dog food.

Lowky looked around the room again; on either side of the fire was a camp bed. They looked so normal, so warm and cosy, that Lowky almost fell asleep just looking at them. There were also two very comfy camp chairs. *This is an oasis*, Lowky thought as he looked at Matilda. Her mouth was slightly open, and Lowky knew he could have blown her over with one small breath. He knew what she was thinking too; it wasn't the food, the water, or even the beds. There was music playing and candles and a lamp! Finally, the silence was broken.

"*Oh my God!* What? How? Wow!" Matilda blurted. Marley smiled. "Ecuadorians are very house proud."

"But the music," Matilda added, flabbergasted

"We own a hardware store; it runs on batteries."

"Can you get a radio? What happened?" Matilda was shaken. It was like she existed again. Her head spun as she struggled to stand.

"For the last two days there has been a bulletin at seven a.m., and then they repeat it at noon and dusk. Other than that, it is just static noise."

Matilda interrupted. "So what happened?" She looked at Lowky, who was sitting with Billy; Billy seemed to be listening intently.

Lowky, on the other hand, heard nothing. He was deep in his thoughts. Life had been so hard but at the same time so simple. Did he really want to know what had happened? It wasn't going to make much difference to him. He knew his mum and sister were dead. Aunt Edie popped into his head.

"Can we hear a news report" Lowky asked.

"No, we've missed the last one for tonight, but you can listen to the new one tomorrow before you head off," Marley suggested to a disappointed Lowky.

"In the meantime, we'll tell you everything we know over dinner," Chilli enthusiastically added. His whole demeanour had changed. He, like the rest of them, was just happy to have someone to talk to. "Marley, have our guests choose their dinner while I make coffee." With that, Chill disappeared behind the pyramid.

Lowky was surprised to see that there was no coffee on the fire. There was, however, a very sophisticated camp oven in which Lowky could see a beautiful loaf browning through the glass lid.

"Over this way." Marley gestured towards the pyramid.

As they walked over, Lowky touched the camp bed and again felt tired.

Matilda got stuck at the oven; she gazed longingly at the bread.

"Help yourselves." Marley gestured to the pile of jars, all individually labelled with people's names and Christmas greetings. To the left of the pyramid were two smaller piles. They were not quite tall enough to be seen over the counter from the other side.

Matilda wandered over curiously.

"Oh those are mine. Dad made them especially," Marley whimsically said as she went on to explain the story of the pickled potions. "They're all delicious, especially with hot bread."

"Really?" Lowky asked, surprised. He leaned over Chilli's pile and read, "Anchovies, sesame seeds, and banana."

"To die for," Chilli responded as he entered the room with a tray of hot coffees.

"Don't say that, Chilli," Marley snapped. "Just don't say it," she added more gently. "Anyway you can pick from the pyramid," she said as she headed back past the counter to the fire.

Lowky moved first and started reading some labels, trying not to giggle. *Mango and mushroom chutney; strawberry and organic dill with buffalo mozzarella jam; dark chocolate, apple, and spinach sauce.* Lowky was baffled. How could any of these taste good?

"Oh, here's one you'll like, Matilda: whipped broccoli, artichoke, and honey swirl."

"Very funny," she spurted. "How about this? Wild oats, orange juice, and potato."

"Yeah, that one's great," Chilli said as he handed them their coffee.

"Here goes," Lowky said as he took a big sip. It was hot and it didn't taste anything like it smelt. "Ahhh," he squealed embarrassingly as he spat it across the floor.

Matilda was more demur; she took a tiny sip but couldn't help screwing up her face.

"Not coffee drinkers then." Chilli laughed as he used a cloth to wipe the floor. "Here, try this." He went back to the tray and grabbed a tube of condensed milk. He squirted half a tube into each cup and stirred in some extra sugar. "Take another sip," he mused, "a little one."

"Oh," Lowky said, surprised. "Not bad." It tasted like muddy sweet milk, but it was warm and energising and he was extremely grateful. "Thank you," he said kindly as Chilli pulled out three biscuits. He gave one to all of them, and Billy was so excited he ate his in one bite.

"Okay, pick your pickle, and let's eat," he said as he grabbed a jar from his pile and went to meet his sister by the fire.

Lowky decide there was no point picking—they all sounded disgusting—so he shut his eyes and grabbed a jar from near the top. He decided not to look at it until he got to the fire.

Matilda was more deliberate. She picked a jar with ingredients she liked, even if they didn't seem to go together. Eventually she left the pyramid with an apricot, cheese, and lightly toasted bacon spread.

They joined up around the fire just as Marley was pulling the bread out the camp oven. As she opened the door the smell reminded Lowky of Saturday mornings at the Overhill Road bakery with his mum and sister. Tushita would always crawl behind the counter and the baker Tom, would give her a cookie.

Marley's bread not only smelled delicious, it looked amazing. It wasn't flat and pale like Lowky's; it was plump and crisp and yum. Before long, Marley ripped off a piece and gave it to him. It was hot in his hands and the steam was warm and comforting. Lowky ripped off a smaller piece and shoved it in his mouth. Matilda did the same.

"Try some pickle," Marley said as she scooped some out of her own jar. "You won't regret it." She shoved the whole piece into her mouth and made silly faces as her eyes rolled back into her head. "Mmmm, try the pickle," she repeated.

"Okay," Lowky said as he bravely looked at the label of his jar. He read it out loud: "What is wild parsley, fig, and limed caviar like?"

"Haven't tried it," Marley replied.

"Me neither," Chill echoed.

"But it will be delicious," they said in unison.

The pickle was unbelievable. It zinged and popped and soothed in a way that was unexplainable. Matilda had just finished placing hers on her bread when Lowky said, "Wow. Can I taste some of yours?"

"Sure." Matilda was glad to have a Guinea pig to try it first.

"Unbelievable," Lowky chimed. "Wow. The apricot, the cheese, the bacon." Lowky smiled uncontrollably. He grabbed the knife and piled some more of his own jar onto his bread. It was like a gift, but it made no sense. Mr. Sal-Henco's pickled potions were truly magical.

CHAPTER 13

○

Islands

L OWKY started on his second cup of coffee as Chilli threw another ball of bread dough into the oven. It had been hidden on a shelf nearby wrapped in a tea towel to rise. Lowky noticed some other loaves there as well and was excited that he might get to pick another jar from the pyramid.

"So," Lowky said. "How do you find yourself here? What's your story?" Chilli went quiet and sat slumped on his bed.

Marley piped up. "On Mondays, Chilli and I walk home from school and meet our dad here. He hates it, but it's the only day he can't get off work early. He's supposed to work till five everyday, but his boss has been very good to him since our mum died." Marley paused and looked off into the distance.

"I'm sorry to hear that," Matilda said soothingly. "I'm starting to understand how it feels. I don't know if my family is alive or dead," she said. *They're alive,* she said to herself as she waited for Marley to go on.

"Once we got home, the earthquake hit—" Marley was interrupted again, this time by Lowky.

"I knew it was an earthquake, but this much damage? It's unreal."

"It was more than an earthquake; The radio guy is calling it the *quake separation*. Apparently, most of Victoria, South Australia, and NSW have been completely separated from the mainland. Those parts have divided into hundreds of waterless islands surrounded by motes of space. Some of the areas nearest to the coast were completely flooded by nine consecutive tsunamis. They are now surrounded by water, which has created a strip of mini islands." Marley took a breath.

"The story changes every day. I don't think anyone really has a clue; like, how would they?" Chilli added defensively.

"That's true, Chilli; it would be hard to get any conclusive information. The splits are also meant to have travelled deep into the mainland. The news said they reached as far as Uluru," Marley added.

"Where are we in all of this?" Matilda asked.

"We're not sure, but we think we might be one of the islands surrounded by air. Chilli and I have both been to the split."

"Really?" Lowky almost squealed. Billy got a shock and barked just for effect.

"Yes." Marley giggled. "We went individually so someone could stay at the store in case Dad came back."

"Well?" Matilda asked. "Can we cross it? How wide is it?"

"It's hard to tell, about fifty metres."

"Forty," Chilli added.

"Whatever really, it's impossible to cross, it's at least fifty metres deep as well. Everything has just fallen in, so even if you could get to the bottom you could never cross it; it's full of debris" Marley checked the bread and then continued. "We were thinking of going the other way."

"Oh, there's no point. I went looking for my mum, and the split on that side is a hundred metres wide. It truly is impossible." Matilda sat forcefully on the bed next to Chilli.

"Don't say that!" Lowky spat. "How does it help? We can't stay here. Eventually we'll all have to leave; even your pyramid won't last forever. There's no point saying what's impossible—tell me what's possible. What else did you see?"

Marley looked up, smiling. "Let's get your beds ready, and I'll tell you all about it over our next loaf of bread."

Lowky nodded, returning the smile, and all five of them got up and started heading down the closest aisle.

"Wow, this place is undamaged," Matilda said. "What happened?"

"Look closely." Chilli smiled.

Matilda and Lowky looked closely at the shelves and their contents. Almost every pallet, pole, can, and tin was dented.

"We have spent the last two weeks cleaning up. All the stuff we couldn't fix we dumped in the nursery and wood yard. I couldn't bear to take you there, it's horrible!" Marley looked around and laughed at her brother. He was more relaxed now as they walked towards the sleeping bags. "This is what's left!" Marley and Chill both picked up identical sleeping bags and handed them to Lowky and Matilda.

"These are the best. They're lightweight, small, and effective," Chilli said as if he was selling the product.

"You can keep them for your journey if you want," Marley added. "They're great for trekking."

Matilda smiled at the twins. "Seriously, I love this place—thank you." She felt safe, happy, and full—oh how the day had changed. Really, she still had nothing, but she was definitely happier.

As they headed back to the main area, Chilli took a left turn through a gap in the shelving. There were camp beds, mattresses, folding chairs, swags, and tents.

"Take what you need," Chilli said, "and if there's anything else, just let us know before morning."

This last statement really upset Matilda, but she didn't say anything. The twins had been very generous and she felt she had no right to be upset.

Lowky was also upset when he realised they only had this evening to get organised. "We have to come up with a plan while we've got the chance," he whispered. "Think big, Matilda; we have about twelve hours to make use of these supplies." Lowky's voice faded as he scanned all the equipment in the aisle.

"First we need to cross the split; no point planning anything else until then," Matilda replied matter-of-factly.

"It's hard to know till we get there, but I'm sure with the right ropes and tools we could cross the bottom," he suggested.

"You can't cross the bottom" Marley, who was innocently walking up ahead, interrupted. "It must be at least fifty metres deep with rubble across the bottom. You'll have to come up with another plan."

"Well, what would you do?" Lowky unintentionally snapped. He looked up at Marley apologetically.

"I would probably try and follow the split around and see if I could find a smaller gap to cross," she replied kindly.

"There are no supplies near the split."

"Well, it's up to you, but that's what I'd do," she finished as she threw them both a lightweight camping mat.

"How far is it from here to the split?" Lowky asked.

"Oh, about a hundred metres. It takes about an hour, though," Marley said.

Lowky started to formulate a very interesting plan.

Lowky and Matilda set up their beds about ten metres away from the twins. They all shared another delicious meal of bread with walnuts and candied goat cheese, and then Matilda and Lowky graciously said their goodnights and slid comfortably into their beds. It was hard not to fall asleep immediately; the bed was like a marshmallow cloud, and Lowky had to pinch himself to stay awake.

"Okay, Matilda, what's the plan?" Lowky asked genuinely.

"We need to unpack everything and start again! There is so much useful stuff here. We only have tomorrow morning, so I think that should be a first priority."

"What do you suggest we replace?" he whispered. "We need the food!"

"Didn't you see the rehydrated food at the top of the aisle near the sleeping bags" Matilda asked, looking at him patiently, but he had not seen it. "Whole meals dehydrated into tiny packets. Perfectly balanced nutritionally." Now Matilda sounded like the salesperson.

"How would you know?" Lowky asked.

"My dad used to buy them whenever my mum went out of town."

"Why not microwave meals?" Lowky asked.

"Come on, Lowky, you remember my dad and microwaves. We never had one in the house, and he didn't want to learn to cook! Some of it was okay though. I always liked the jerky."

"What's jerky?" he asked.

"Dried-out meat." Matilda smiled

"Ohh! Sounds delicious." Lowky rolled his eyes.

"Anyway, it's stupid carrying cans when we can carry ten times as much of this other stuff."

"Okay, but what about the split? What do you want to do?"

"No clue, except to climb into it. It can't be impossible, and the twins don't know what we've crossed already. They don't know what we're capable of." Matilda seemed convinced by this argument and started making a list. "We'll definitely need rope and latches and maybe some type of platform—"

Lowky interrupted. "We need to go look at it, Matilda. From what Marley said, there is no point planning a descent if it's impossible."

"How are we going to do that? We have to leave by morning, and it's stupid not to pack anything from here."

"We need to ask the twins for one more day. If they say no . . . we'll take two ropes and as much dehydrated food and water as possible." Lowky stopped to think for a second. "We can grab two of those really good lightweight packs and save our good small pack to somehow transport Billy."

"Oh shit, Billy!" Matilda snorted. "How is that going to work?"

"Well, we'll have to hoist or carry him in some way," Lowky suggested. "Maybe there's a camping section for pets."

"And what if they let us stay another day? Then what?"

"We just need to go and check out the split. We should both go so we know what we're dealing with."

"I'll go with you, no problems, but you can ask the twins." Matilda yawned. "I don't like your chances, though; they made it pretty clear we have to leave."

"You got any better ideas?" Lowky asked defensively.

"No ideas at all! We need to sleep. We'll think better in the morning, and if they kick us out in a hurry, we know what to grab."

Lowky reluctantly agreed. He shut his eyes and was gone.

CHAPTER 14

Extension

L OWKY woke to the smell of coffee wrapping around him like his mother's arms. At that exact moment he had both a vision of the past and the future and he was at peace. They just had to find a way to cross the split.

Lowky frantically wanted to start planning. He looked over at Matilda, but she was gone. On her bed were two ropes, four carabineers, and four packets of dehydrated pasta with mushroom. Lowky lay there wondering if the twins would let them take just one more jar of their dad's magical concoctions.

It wasn't long at all before curiosity got Lowky out of bed. He shuffled, still half asleep, into the "living room." Everyone was already there. He looked at a surprisingly clean Matilda.

She smiled at him as she took another forkful of what looked like pancakes.

"Pancakes?!" Lowky asked with both surprise and delight.

"Uh huh," Matilda said. "You want some?" she asked mockingly.

Lowky didn't have to respond. Matilda took two thick pancakes off a stack that was keeping warm near the fire. "There's honey!"

Lowky sat down happily and consciously decided not to worry. He drizzled a restrained amount of honey over his breakfast.

"I was talking to Matilda and suggested you guys might want to stay another day just to get organised. What do you think?" Marley asked.

"Oh, that would be great," Lowky said as he flashed Matilda a look. Had she asked them? He couldn't imagine it. "Are you sure it's okay?"

"It's okay." Marley smiled warmly.

"Are you ready for another adventure?" Lowky said as he bent down to pat Billy.

Billy looked up enthusiastically as he licked the last bit of honey pancake off his lip.

"What about you, Matilda, do you want to come?" He hesitated. "I think you should."

"Where are you headed?" Chilli asked suspiciously.

"To the split. Our only chance is to cross it, and to do that we need to know what we're up against" Lowky looked at Chilli for a clue.

"Why don't we all go?" Marley piped in.

"What if Dad comes!" Chilli snapped. "Someone has to stay."

"Come on, Chilli, we'll leave a note; we won't be gone for long."

"*No!*" Chilli screamed. "Someone has to stay!"

"Okay, okay," Marley said calmly as she headed towards a distraught Chilli. He threw his plate in her direction and stormed off towards the aisles.

Marley turned to look at Lowky and Matilda. "You two better go. I'll get a nice lunch ready for when you get back." She pulled out a small loaf of bread and said, "Here, take this." She looked sadly towards the aisles, smiled at her visitors, and walked away.

Lowky looked at Matilda and Billy, still a motley crew. "It's hard to imagine that just three weeks ago we could have driven home."

"Yeah, and we could have done it in ten minutes." Matilda laughed.

"Yeah, we haven't travelled far."

"Who cares?" Matilda smiled. "Come on, Lowky, this is a minor miracle, this place. I haven't eaten like this since the quake."

"Oh no! What time is it?" Lowky shouted as he turned and ran back into the store.

"How am I supposed to know?" Matilda who was hurrying to catch up yelled. "What's going on?"

"The news—how could we forget the news!" Lowky was frantic as he entered the living room to look for the solar-powered camp alarm. It had been on the counter the night before.

"Where is it?" he cried as he shuffled through the stuff on the counter.

"Stop it, Lowky. You know what the twins are like."

"Well where is it?" Lowky demanded.

"Probably out in the sun." Matilda giggled but Lowky wasn't in the mood.

"It's the news, Matilda, don't you want to know? Aren't you curious how this happened?"

"I know the basics" Matilda mumbled.

"Shhhh," Lowky whispered. "What's that?"

They both stopped in their tracks and listened.

It was Chilli, and he was still crying.

"Do you think we should just turn the radio on?"

"No, Lowky. Really, they've been kind enough and we want to stay the night, don't we? We don't even know what time it is, but I'm sure it's after seven." Matilda paused. "If we leave now, maybe we can catch the repeat broadcast at midday."

"But how will we know? We don't know the time."

"Who cares?" Matilda snapped. "It's on again tonight!" She was rarely upset, but when she was, well—watch out. She turned around and stormed out the front window.

Billy looked at Lowky and reluctantly but wisely followed Matilda.

What just happened? he thought while still attempting to look for the clock. In fewer than five minutes he had gone from standing out in the sun, ready to carry out a new mission to crazed, angry, ungrateful villain. He stopped looking for the clock and came out of the window towards Matilda; he had intended to apologise, but he didn't need to. Matilda was already standing in the sun, smiling.

CHAPTER 15

○

Possible

IT took a casual two hours to get to the split. Matilda and Lowky laughed most of the way and forgot about the terrain that they were now accustomed to. Billy reached there first. They had known they were close from the last rise they had crossed, but now they were in a gully of rubble, following Billy.

Once Billy reached the top, he barked uncontrollably, and Matilda and Lowky frantically called him back in case the SES was there. In true Billy style he ignored them and disappeared over the other side. It was a tall, daunting pile and both Lowky and Matilda looked at it.

"It looks like it used to be a house," Lowky mused as he started to climb.

"It doesn't look like it used to be anything," Matilda replied as she cautiously attempted the first layer of broken rock.

They walked tentatively. Billy had stopped barking, and they had no idea what awaited them on the other side.

Matilda arrived at the top first; she had overtaken Lowky at the very first opportunity and was now waiting patiently for him just before the summit. When Lowky finally arrived, they looked at each other nervously.

"I'll take a look," Matilda suggested with very little choice.

"Okay, okay," Lowky interrupted out of pride. "We'll look together on the count of three."

Matilda slowly and purposely started counting. "One . . . two . . . three."

They popped their heads up together. The split was bigger than they ever could have imagined, and Marley's word *impossible* kept playing in Lowky's head. What was more surprising was the five-metre gap between them and the split. It was almost flattened. Some parts were smooth to the dirt and from their high vantage point you could see that the force had caused everything close to the edge to slide in, leaving nothing behind. Billy was sitting on one of the smooth areas, comfortably licking himself.

"It's not fifty metres," Matilda said optimistically.

Lowky looked at her surprised as he tried to work out what she was talking about.

"The split—it's not fifty metres, wide or deep."

She was right. The gap was more like thirty metres, but it was hard to tell.

"Marley was right; we can't go in," Lowky said, looking at Matilda but she was clearly lost in thought. "I've got an idea," he added. "Let's go across the top."

"You're joking." Matilda said, choking with laughter.

"No, I'm not. Have you got any other suggestions?"

"We just have to find another place to cross, clearly!"

"No, we don't. Just listen."

Matilda sat on a smooth patch next to Billy, nodding.

"Look, we have the store, so we have access to almost anything we could need. I suggest we tie some ladders together and cross that way."

Matilda stopped nodding for a second and thought seriously. 'Wouldn't it break in the middle with our weight?"

"No. It would bend and wobble, but it shouldn't break." He looked at Matilda as she contemplated the idea. "We could wrap and tie the joints with heaps of rope to make it more secure, and we would go one at a time and then use a pulley to get our bags and Billy to the other side."

"How would we get all the equipment here?" Matilda asked, working out the details.

"We'll have to do a few loads," he said proudly. "We could do two tonight so that we can leave first thing in the morning. I'm sure the twins would help."

"Okay, Mr. Tick, I have to admit, that's not a bad idea. Why don't we do some planning over lunch?" She reached into her backpack to pull out the bread Marley had given her earlier, and to her surprise she felt something cold against her fingers. "Oh my God!" she squealed. "Gingerbread, oranges, and mashed potato pickle."

A smile spread across Lowky's face. He sat down to join Matilda as she pulled off two big hunks of bread and handed them both to Lowky. She reached over and grabbed a shard of strewn plastic to use as a knife and generously smothered the bread with what she knew would be divine. She unashamedly took the larger slice of bread and took a bite. Her eyes rolled back in her head as the magic slid down her throat.

"Those twins *are* maniacs." She laughed. "I wouldn't share this with anyone."

Lowky reached into a small pack he had taken from the store and pulled out his little black book.

"Hey, where did you get that? It's mine!" Matilda screamed as she leapt over to grab it.

"Hey, stop, do you want to fall in there?" Lowky ordered as he grabbed her with one hand and pointed to the split with the other.

"But that's my book, Lowky, it's all I've got," she exclaimed as she carefully pulled herself back towards the rubble. Her voice was shaking. There was no smile.

"No it's not, Matilda," he quickly explained. "I picked it up from the IGA. I was going to surprise you but then I used it to write a note for Sam, and since then I've been writing down heaps of stuff. Look, here are the plans from last night." Lowky handed the book to her like a peace offering.

She looked through it suspiciously but soon realised it wasn't hers. "Well." She giggled nervously. "You could still give it to me."

"No way, you bully!" Lowky teased. "You almost killed me. Anyway, I like it now, and you have enough already." He snatched the book back out of her hand. "Where was I?" He opened the book and wrote messily at the top.

> Split Supplies
> 3 x ladders
> At least 6 long, strong ropes
> 2 x climbing harnesses
> 4 x carabineers
> A way to carry Billy
> A way to carry supplies

Once Lowky finished his first list, he started another one:

> Transporting Billy

He looked up at Matilda and led with his usual "got any ideas?"

"I have, actually. I've been thinking about it all night," she answered enthusiastically.

"And . . . ?"

"*And* . . . the twins are bound to have a baby carrier for trekking, something strong and lightweight. If we find one that you carry on the front, we can put his back paws through the hole like baby's feet."

Lowky looked at her curiously as she continued. "His front paws could hang out the top, and we could tie the carrier to me just for extra safety."

"I'm glad you're carrying him." Lowky laughed at the image.

"We all know you won't. I'll be surprised if you make it across at all," she teased.

Lowky had to admit it was an excellent idea, and he couldn't help but grin as he went back to his book:

> Transporting Billy
> 1x baby carrier
> More rope

Lowky started another list as Matilda watched over his shoulder.

Carrying supplies

He looked at Matilda again, but she had nothing.

"The way I see it," he said, "we have two options."

Matilda looked at him curiously.

"Option one—we could do multiple trips" Matilda laughed. "Or option two," Lowky continued, "we set up a pulley system."

"And how do you suppose we do that?" she asked mockingly.

"It shouldn't be too hard," he stated proudly as he leant over to draw her a picture. "All we have to do is tie a very large rope around the rungs of the ladders and then pull it along." He pointed to the diagram.

"Well, it's better than option one," she conceded as she devoured the rest of the bread and then packed up the utensils. She carefully hid what was left of the pickles in the bottom of her bag so they could pretend they had eaten it all. It would be a welcome treat later in the journey.

Lowky sat quietly and reluctantly shared his bread with Billy. He wasn't overly hungry but didn't want to waste the pickle. Lowky watched Billy intently; as Billy swallowed the bread he closed his eyes. On his second mouthful, he ate more slowly and savoured every chew. Even Billy seemed to appreciate the magic of Mr. Sal-Henco's pickles.

The group arrived back delighted, and it only got better. The entrance smelled of a feast and they tripped over each other trying to get to the living room. Chilli was stoking the fire with one hand and eating vegemite toast with the other.

"Vegemite toast!" Lowky exclaimed. "Really?"

"There's a plate of them over there—help yourself." Chilli laughed.

Lowky got there first and grabbed a slice from the top of the pile. He, like Billy, cherished every mouthful. Matilda wasn't far behind and they looked at each other gratefully.

"Make the most of it, Matilda," Lowky whispered. "Things are soon to change."

They spent the rest of the afternoon talking to the twins about their ideas. With every conversation either Marley or Chilli would wonder off and come back with what they needed. First it was lightweight backpacks, then rope, and then a baby carrier.

"You'll have to help me with the ladders, but it's no problem; we have three that are three metres long," Marley said.

"That should more than cover it," Chilli said as he came back with an armful of lightweight clothes. "We'll help you carry all this stuff to the split, but then you're on your own."

"Thanks, Chilli," Lowky and Matilda said in unison.

The rest of the afternoon was spent eating, packing, and repacking. In the end they got rid of all their mismatched clothes and replaced them with top-quality trekking gear. The twins generously gave them ten packs of dehydrated food, two jars of pickles, a packet of flour, and as much water as they could carry.

"Sorry we can't give you any more," Marley said sadly, "but we need our food—who knows how long we'll be here?"

Lowky smiled gratefully as he sorted through the food they had bought from home. They seemed to have more room now, and he made a new list of supplies in his little black book.

Lowky and Matilda looked around, satisfied they had packed all they could. Matilda had the pack with the clothes, bedding, and half the food. Lowky had the rest of the food and the water. They had also collected a couple of books, one on Bush Tucker plants and one on cultivating vegetable gardens. Lowky carried the books in a front pack, with a large tarp they could use for shelter. They twins also loaded them up with a radio, torches, and a very small army stove with kerosene for fuel. Matilda and Lowky argued for a while about carrying it.

"We can just start a fire, Matilda," Lowky insisted.

"Yeah, and what if we can't?" Matilda retaliated. Eventually she won, and Lowky added the stove to his pack. Marley also bought him a brand new toastie iron but he kept his—it was burnt with memories. Matilda filled the baby carrier with some random items and used gaffer tape to close off the legs. She threw the gaffer into the carrier and sat on her bed, satisfied.

"It's five to four," Marley yelled from the living room. "Did you guys want to hear the news?"

CHAPTER 16

News

T HEY all sat around the radio in anticipation. The twins had not yet heard the daily news and they too were excited to hear the latest developments. For a while all they heard was static, and then the radio clicked and what sounded like a very young man started to speak. Matilda cried immediately. They had not been connected to anything outside themselves for what seemed like an eternity, and just for a second everything felt normal.

The young man was clearly not a news reader but he was trying his hardest. It occurred to Lowky that he probably had no idea whether anyone was listening. *We're listening,* Lowky thought as they all sat silently around the radio.

"Good morning. I'm pretty sure today is the thirteenth of September, eleven days since the earthquake. The news has not changed much; it is still my understanding that most of NSW, Victoria, and SA have been destroyed. This has created numerous islands of land, separated by massive gashes. Some islands are surrounded by trapped water from the tsunamis that followed the earthquake. Helicopters have managed to get to some islands but cannot land. There has been some news that the helicopters are dropping supplies and emergency workers to some of the islands. It is impossible to leave most of the island as they are completely isolated by the separation from the mainland. Some rescues have taken place, but a lot of people who survived the earthquake and tsunamis are now dying from injuries or starvation. I myself have not seen a helicopter yet, but I am hoping to. Until tomorrow, good luck and farewell."

Lowky and Matilda just looked at each other. Lowky felt the fear setting in as the elation from the morning completely disappeared. What if there are more splits that they have to cross? *What if the farm has been completely destroyed? What if . . .* Lowky was interrupted by that little voice inside that kindly said, *What if everything is okay?* He tried to smile as Marley handed him a cup of pumpkin soup.

"Pumpkin soup!" Lowky exclaimed. "Really?" Everyone laughed as they shared campfire stories and enjoyed the rest of their time together. It was soon time for bed, as Lowky and Matilda intended on leaving early the next morning.

Morning came quickly, and Lowky could see he was not the only one reluctant to leave. Matilda stayed as long as possible in the warmth and comfort of her bed, but eventually the smells from the living room enticed her to move. They all ate a nourishing and delicious bowl of muesli with dried fruit, and Chilli came from behind the counter with a hot pot of coffee. Lowky had become quite accustomed to the taste. In fact, you could even say he enjoyed it. Matilda, on the other hand, really struggled and had to put three, four, sometimes five teaspoons of sugar in so she could drink it. It wasn't her favourite thing but she definitely wasn't going to say no to something warm and sweet. Chilli handed Lowky a bag of coffee, a small camping percolator, three small UHT milks, and a small bag of sugar for Matilda.

After breakfast, they all walked slowly to the front window, picked up the supplies, and headed to the split.

CHAPTER 17

Casualties

THE trip to the split was surprisingly easy. The ladders were more of a help than a hindrance. One of the major advantages was that when they got to large piles of rubble, they could use them to climb over. This was no help to Billy, of course, but then again Billy needed no help.

Marley and Chilli carried two of the ladders, one in each hand, Marley at the front and Chilli at the back. Chilli wore a small backpack and Marley carried the baby carrier for Matilda. Lowky and Matilda shared a ladder, and the four chatted easily as they crossed the last pile of rubble before the split.

Chilli opened his backpack and pulled out a camp stove, rather larger than the one he had given them. He started percolating coffee and making flat bread while the other three got to work on the ladders. The girls bound the ends of each ladder together with rope while Lowky came behind and tied the knots.

"I knew Scouts would come in handy for something," he said as he thought about all the boys in his group and wondered if they too were using the skills they'd been taught. Within twenty minutes their ladder bridge was ready. It lay flat for sixty metres, and Lowky suddenly wondered how they would get it to lie across the top. He sat quietly working on the pulley system while he tried to come up with a plan.

"You're just going to have to stand it up on its feet and drop it over the split and hope for the best," Chilli said, as if reading his mind.

"I just don't know if we'll have the strength to stand it on its feet," Lowky said intensely.

It's not about strength or balance," Chilli replied. "We won't have enough of either, but we will be able to tip it. It's fairly long, so even if it goes askew it should still reach the other side."

"No point talking about it," Lowky grumbled. "Once I've got the pulley system on, we'll give it a try."

They hardly spoke over lunch as they reflected on the relationships that had developed over two short days. Lowky felt as if he had known the twins forever, and the "maniacs" they had first encountered seemed like a dream from another lifetime. Lowky sat quietly counting his blessings.

They took a long time eating and then started chatting. Lowky was trying to drag out their time together, but eventually Matilda stood up and said, "Let's do this thing."

They all manoeuvred the ridiculously oversized ladder back towards the last pile of rubble. It sat precariously on top, like a seesaw. It was only just weighted to the side of the split, but it was ready to tip at any moment. Everyone held on to the ladder to ensure it stayed in position.

Marley and Chilli stood on one side and Lowky and Matilda stood on the other. In unison they all tried lifting the ladder above their heads and walking it back up the rubble.

"If only we could get higher," Lowky said, exasperated.

"Well, we can't," Chilli said in his annoying, matter-of-fact way.

"Any ideas, then?" Lowky snapped as he tried again to lift the ladder above his head.

"Yeah, actually, I think if someone got us started up here and the other three tried to get under the ladder from the bottom and push it, we just might be able to get it to its feet."

Lowky had to admit it was a good idea, and he humbly lowered the ladder.

"You or me?" Lowky asked more kindly.

"You're taller than me, so you stay up here and I'll go to the bottom. If it doesn't work, we can always swap over."

Lowky agreed, and Chilli headed to the bottom of the rubble to tell the girls the plan.

"One . . . two . . . three!" Matilda screamed towards Lowky once they were all in position.

Lowky lifted the ladder above his head. His arms were shaking but he refused to let go.

Matilda quickly manoeuvred herself under the ladder and walked towards it. Lowky scrambled down the rubble while trying to keep the ladder above his head, and at the same time the twins stayed at the bottom, trying to manipulate the ladder from their end. Eventually, as the ladder got higher, Lowky had to let go. He literally rolled down the hill to try and help the others at the bottom, but it was too late.

"Heads up!" Chilli screamed as the ladder came thumping back down on the rubble.

Matilda just managed to dive out of the way before it landed on her. She then flipped over just in time to grab the bottom of the ladder before it seesawed to the other side.

"Not bad," Marley said optimistically. "We should get it next time."

Lowky was unreasonably frustrated and had to control his urge to push Marley into the split.

Matilda was also frustrated and the most bruised and battered of the group and flashed Lowky a "shut up" smile. "Why don't you go check the knots before we start again?" she insisted.

Lowky nodded and headed quietly back up the rubble. The knots had held up perfectly, and although he could not check them all, he was confident they were fine. Once he was back on top of the pile, he yelled down to the others. "Ready when you are."

"Ready!" Matilda screamed, and the process started again.

This time Lowky had found a large piece of wood, and he used it to push the ladder even further above his head. As he negotiated the rubble, he quickly moved the wood to a lower rung, narrowly missing on a number of occasions. As the ladder got to the three-quarter mark, they could feel they were starting to lose control of it again. It was too top heavy, and they just didn't have the strength to tip it over.

"Heads up!" Chilli screamed as he lost his balance and had to let go.

This time Lowky couldn't move fast enough and the ladder came crashing down on the back of his legs. "Ahhhh!" he screamed as he tried to wiggle his legs out. "A little help here!" he cried.

Everyone ran towards him, and within a few seconds they had lifted the ladder enough for him to escape. Lowky's legs were cut and bleeding, but nothing was broken. He used one the super absorbent towels they had picked up from the hardware store to cover the wounds. Matilda and Marley helped him hobble back to the smooth space before the split.

They all sat around the cooker feeling pretty hopeless as Marley showed Matilda how to make a good pot of coffee.

"We need another plan," Matilda said as she spooned the coffee into the percolator. "This one clearly isn't working."

They all agreed but sat dumbfounded about what to do next. Marley started to move towards the stove, and as she did she accidently kicked one of the ropes. It started rolling towards the split, unwinding and unravelling as it went. Marley jumped on it just in time. Most of it had remained on the ledge, but a long piece was hanging over the side.

"I have an idea." Marley smiled calmly, still lying flat and spread-eagle on top of the rope. They all looked at her blankly.

"Go on," Lowky said curiously.

"Well, what if two of us push and two of us pull? We could tie one end of this rope to one of the top rungs and pull it from this side while two people push it from underneath." Marley smiled, as the idea flowed from her and she realised it was actually a pretty good one.

"It's worth a try," Matilda said.

"Good one, Sis" Chilli added as they all turned to look at Lowky.

"I'm in," he mumbled, "but someone else can go under the ladder this time."

"I'll do it," Matilda said happily as she grabbed the rope and started climbing back up the rubble.

"Don't you want your coffee?" Marley asked.

"No, later. I just want to get this done."

They all got into position. Matilda tied the rope as high up the ladder as she could without making it seesaw to the other side. Her knots weren't as good as Lowky's but it would do. She threw the rope to the bottom, and Marley and Lowky pulled it until it was taut. Chilli sat at the bottom, ready to get under the ladder as soon as it was high enough off the rubble.

"One . . . two . . . three!" Matilda screamed, and the process started all over again. This time it was easier. Matilda missed the rung once with the piece of wood but it was okay because the rope held the ladder in place just long enough for her to get back into position. They had the ladder at about eighty degrees and only needed to get it up a little bit further, but Matilda and Marley were running out of room. Chilli and Matilda were pushing with all their might.

"Come on, come on!" Matilda screamed. "We're so close, just a little further," but it was no use, the ladder was just too big and they were just too small.

At that moment, Billy, who had been sitting halfway up the rubble ran towards the ladder and leaped with all his might. His shoulder and torso hit the ladder as if he was executing a rugby tackle. This pushed it until it was almost vertical. The kids at the bottom gave it one final heave, and for a microsecond the ladder was standing on its feet, teetering on the precipice of the other side.

"Keep pushing!" they all screamed until finally the ladders were over and crashing across the split. They waited silently as the dust settled, and amazingly the ladders lay in front of them almost flat across the top.

"I can't believe it!" Matilda screamed.

"Way to go!" Marley yelled excitedly.

"You rock, Billy Baxter!" Lowky smiled as he turned around to pat him. "Billy!" he screamed. They all turned to see Billy lying motionless on the smooth surface between the rubble and the split.

Everyone started crying and screaming and running all at the same time. Lowky got to Billy first and patted him gently on the face. He ripped of his T-shirt and placed it under his head to stop the blood that was draining from a large gash. He felt the warmth of Billy's breath on his arm.

"He's still breathing!" he yelled to the others. "Get water and a blanket." Lowky snatched the water from Matilda and dabbed a bit on the corner of his T-shirt to clean Billy's wound. Billy opened his eyes slightly and Lowky helped him lift his head so he could take a drink.

"He seems all right," Lowky said, "just knocked himself out I think."

Slowly and carefully Lowky squeezed Billy's legs and body. He let out a little weak bark as Lowky touched his front ankle, but it didn't seem to be broken. With great love, Lowky wrapped Billy in a sleeping bag and carried him over to the camp stove. Billy lay comfortably in Lowky's arms as the others ran around trying to help as best they could.

"We'll have to stay here tonight, Matilda," Lowky said seriously as he glanced at Billy. "We can't take him across like this."

Matilda agreed as she tore Lowky's T-shirt into strips to make a bandage.

"You could come back with us," Marley said as she looked at Chilli. He nodded supportively.

"Nah, thanks anyway." Lowky smiled. "We'll have to get moving as early as possible tomorrow; we can't afford to lose another day."

"Fair enough." Marley smiled. "At least let me make you something to eat before we leave."

She cooked up some of the dehydrated pasta and handed it to Lowky and Matilda.

"Aren't you eating?" Matilda asked. "You must be starving."

"No, we'll eat at home. Who knows how long your supplies will last?" She looked towards the sun, which was already halfway to the horizon. "We should head off, Chilli" she said kindly. "It will take a while to get home, especially without the ladders."

Chill agreed and they both reluctantly stood up to leave.

Matilda jumped to her feet to hug them both goodbye.

Lowky couldn't move and didn't want to disturb the now sleeping Billy, so they hugged him warmly and turned away. "We can't thank you enough," he said shyly. "Really, thank you."

The twins started to climb the rubble, and at the top they turned one last time to wave goodbye.

Lowky and Matilda were silent for a long time. Lowky sat with Billy, smothering him with love while Matilda got a fire ready to keep them warm. She organised the beds and made a saucepan of lemon tea, but they were both asleep before they could drink it.

CHAPTER 18

Crossing

Lowky woke up, frantic. He couldn't feel Billy at his feet. He'd had an old cat once that had disappeared and his mum told him that sick animals often go away to die. *Has Billy died?*

Matilda was still asleep as Lowky squirmed out of his sleeping bag and turned around. There was Billy, as if nothing had happened, drinking the lemon tea out of the cooker. Lowky laughed, mainly from the relief but also because Billy looked so comical. Lowky's yellow T-shirt had shifted out of place overnight and part of it was now covering his left eye.

Lowky ran over and warmly hugged him. "You gave me a good scare, Dog," he said lovingly, "but you fixed the ladder, see!"

Billy started to walk towards the split, and Lowky could see that he was still sore and limping, but he was alive and moving and that was good enough. He poured the rest of the lemon tea into Billy's bowl and started to prepare coffee. He made it weak to see if Matilda would like it better. As the smell of coffee started to coat the air, Matilda's eyes opened and she smiled at the two boys standing side by side.

"Come here, Billy," she beamed as he limped over to her. "Good boy."

Billy curled up in a space on her sleeping bag and fell back asleep.

The sky was awash with the colour of sunrise as the first rays of light hit the clouds. They were clouds all right—big, menacing clouds—and

Lowky realised it hadn't rained since their journey began; amazing for Melbourne.

"That's it, Matilda, let's move. We'll drink this coffee, but let's eat on the other side. The rain's coming and well never get across *this* in the rain." Lowky was never wrong about the rain; it was a gift, really. If Lowky said the rain was coming, then the rain was coming. Even if the sky was blue you took a raincoat if Lowky told you to.

"Okay, I'll go first with Billy," Matilda said as she sat up and rubbed her eyes.

"Are you sure? It's dangerous—maybe I should go first to see how strong it is before we put extra weight on it? I can check and tighten the knots that way."

"Okay, you go first, but I thought you were scared of heights."

"I am," Lowky said, trying not to think about it, "but that's not going to change today." He had his last sip of coffee and packed it into his pack, and he cleaned up the rest of the mess and did the same.

"Wow," Matilda said genuinely, "I must be getting used to this coffee. I only needed one spoon of sugar."

Lowky smiled but didn't say anything as time was short and the clouds were quickly getting angry.

*

Lowky steadied himself. At any other time this would have been an impossible feat. He took a deep breath and shut his eyes.

"You got the walkie-talkie?" Matilda asked.

"Check."

"And some water and food just in case?"

"There is no 'just in case,' Matilda," he said firmly, "but yes, check, I have water, food, and a lighter."

"Okay. Once you get to the other side, 'talkie me and I'll attach our packs to the pulley system, then I'll come over with Billy." She was taking the stuff out of the baby carrier and trying to fit it into the other packs.

"Just make sure you hold this end of the ladder," he said fearfully. "Once I've crossed, put rocks on this end so there some support for you when you cross."

"Come on, Lowky, stop wasting time; I'll take care of this end, don't worry!"

"And Billy."

"Of course."

"I love you, Matilda," he said softly. "You're my best friend."

Matilda looked up, surprised. "I love you too, Lowky. Now get on the ladder."

The wind was already starting to pick up, and Lowky took a deep breath as he got onto his hands and knees. He tested the ladder with his hands and realised how unstable it was. It immediately started to sink and shake. *Okay, here goes nothing . . .* Lowky thought but heard his mum in his head: *Careful what you wish for, Lowky,* and he immediately changed his words: *All is well.*

Before he knew it he was over the edge and kneeling on the ladder in mid-air. *You're a fool, Lowky, all is well, all is well.* He made it to the next rung. *All is well, all is well,* and another and another.

What sort of idiot . . . . He looked down at his elbows as they started to shake. *All is well, all is well,* another rung and another. Lowky had his eyes closed as often as possible and was surprised when he felt rope under his fingertips. He had made it to the end of the first ladder.

He could hear Matilda's voice in the background but whatever it was, it would have to wait. The ladder was drooping significantly and the wind was starting to cause it to sway. Lowky was sweating and shaking and crying and couldn't move any further. He was frozen. That little internal voice with its comforting tone stepped in when he could not. *All is well, Lowky,* it said calmly, *keep moving.*

In the meantime, the sinking of the ladder had caused it to move significantly. Matilda had been trying to hold it with all her might, but it was almost at the edge of the split and about to fall in. Matilda screamed as she tried desperately to bring the ladder back.

This sent Lowky into a spin. He had not expected the ladder to jolt underneath him, and he thought for a second that something had gone wrong. At that point all he wanted to do was stay still and hold on, but he knew no one could help him but himself. He found something deep inside him and resolutely manoeuvred his hand to the next rung. He shut his eyes again. *All is well, all is well.*

As Lowky moved so did the ladder, but luckily he didn't know it. Matilda could see Lowky was close but just couldn't judge how far he had to go.

"Come on, Lowky, hurry," she whispered as the rope slipped a little from her grip. "Come on, Lowky!" she screamed, not because he could hear her but because it gave her strength.

Lowky moved more confidently, and with his eyes shut he was making better progress. Again he was surprised when he felt the rope that joined the next two ladders together. He opened his eyes, and to his delight he was only a few rungs from the other side.

Matilda couldn't do it anymore and was about to let go when Billy barked and grabbed the rope with his teeth. At the same time, Lowky moved forward, and four rungs later he was still on the ladder but over solid ground. He wasted no time getting off.

Matilda and Billy went flying as the weight shifted and the ladder came hurtling back towards them. Lowky had no idea what had happened, but he was glad he was off the ladder when it did. He searched through his small pack for the walkie-talkie and turned it on.

"What's going on over there? Matilda, Matilda, come in, Matilda." He waited a minute but both Matilda and Billy were lying exhausted on the ground. "Everything okay at your end, Matilda?" he said, starting to worry.

Matilda crawled breathlessly to the walkie-talkie and hit the button. "No problems here, Lowky," she said, laughing to herself. "How was it?"

"Scary, scary, just shut your eyes and don't look down, I don't know how you're going to go with Billy. The ladders slumped a lot just under my weight."

"Oh, while you're on that subject, how much ladder do you have on that side?"

"Almost a whole one—the split must be only about forty metres wide."

"*Only* forty metres? Oh, is that all!" Matilda replied sarcastically. "Can you try and push it back a little and jam it up against something there so it doesn't slip forward?"

Lowky didn't bother asking any questions; he put his walkie-talkie down and pushed the ladder about ten metres towards the split. Then he jammed it into a large slab of cement.

"Done," he said as the walkie-talkie crackled.

"Great. I'll attach the carabineer to a backpack and then you can pull it across."

"Okey dokey," he replied optimistically.

While he was waiting for Matilda, he looked around. It was much like the other side: a smooth space of about three metres before a massive pile of destruction.

"Okay ready to go" Lowky heard through his walkie-talkie. Lowky started to pull but immediately ran into a problem. The rope wouldn't move. He tried again but then realised the rope had been attached to the ends of the ladder bridge and were now squashed between the ladder and the dirt. Lowky tried again but it wouldn't budge.

"Matilda, you're going to have to unlatch the backpack and tie the rope at the first rung over the split. It won't move."

"What?" she asked, tired and annoyed. The wind was becoming frantic and her own fears about crossing the split with a dog weren't helping.

"The rope is stuck between the ladder and the dirt. It won't move. Go to the edge and retie it so it can hang freely, and let me know when you're finished."

"I don't know if my knot will be strong enough."

"All is well, Matilda," he said, trying to be supportive, but Matilda got angry and turned the walkie-talkie off as violently as possible without breaking it. She got up half-heartedly but was determined not to cross this thing in the rain.

"All right, ready," she sighed once she had tied the rope and turned the walkie-talkie back on.

"Great. Let's try this again. You attach the backpack and I'll pull."

"Done," Matilda said after a few minutes.

Lowky felt invincible after the ladder experience, but it was only a few seconds before he realised there was another problem. He pulled and pulled, but all that happened was that the backpack kept banging into the cliff near Matilda. It was going in the wrong direction. The only way Lowky could pull the supplies over was from underneath the ladder, and that was impossible. He walked tentatively over to the walkie-talkie.

"Matilda."

"I know," she complained. "I'm not an idiot."

"You're going to have to pull it."

"I said I know," she snapped and again turned off the walkie-talkie. After everything that had happened, Matilda wondered how she would have the energy to cross the split, but she moved quickly and was sitting on the edge with the rope in her hand. The first pack was filled with clothes and camping stuff and was the lighter of the two. She began to pull, and to her surprise the pack started to move smoothly and quickly towards the other side. Within a few minutes she felt the pack stop and wondered if it had reached its destination.

She quickly leaned over and turned the walkie-talkie back on, just in time to hear Lowky say, "Got it!"

She attached the other pack with a new carabineer. It was much heavier than the last one, and she had to balance precariously on the edge to get it in place. This pack moved a little slower because of the weight, but before long, it too was at the other side.

"Got it," Lowky said excitedly.

"Be careful; it's much heavier."

"Will do," he replied cheerfully.

"God you're annoying," she said but this time she kept the walkie-talkie on.

Putting Billy in the baby carrier was hysterical, and any other time Matilda would have laughed, but not today. She tried to be careful of his injuries, but Billy was being far from helpful and eventually she just had to pick him up and force him in. He stood comically, with his butt in the carrier, and even Matilda managed a little smile. She tied a thin piece of rope to the carrier and then across both his shoulders to ensure he wouldn't fall out the top. She took a deep breath.

"Okay, Lowky, I'm on my way," she said nervously. There was no one to hold the ladder for her, but if Lowky could make it, she certainly could. She picked up the carrier and put it on her front so Billy wasn't upside down. It didn't matter though; he kicked and squirmed and growled and even attempted to bite her. She picked up the transmitter and dumped Billy back on the ground. He wasn't happy.

"I can't do this," she said into the transmitter.

"Why? I checked all the knots, and it's not that bad. Just shut your eyes as much as possible. I've started a nice fire over here—but hurry, Matilda, I think it's starting to rain."

"It's not me," she snapped defensively. "It's Billy, he's okay on the ground but as soon as I try to put the carrier on, he goes crazy. I'll never be able to cross with him carrying on like that."

"Oh, shit! Give me a minute," Lowky replied. He had never been able to make decisions quickly, and sometimes he couldn't make them at all.

Matilda interrupted his thoughts. "I'm sending him over on the pulley. I'll pull the rope over first so you can check the knots, but be quick. I'm not crossing in the rain."

Lowky wanted to protest for Billy's safety. He tried desperately to think of another idea but had nothing, so he reluctantly agreed. Lowky thoroughly checked the knots and then gave Matilda the okay.

"I'll pull him across as fast as I can. He's not going to like it, so watch he doesn't bite you when you try and get him out. I'll come over as soon as you've got him, so be ready." She looked compassionately at Billy as she felt the first drops of rain on her face.

"Okay, Billy, suck it up," she said firmly. She quickly picked him up from the back of the carrier, trying to keep his teeth as far away as possible. She lowered him to the carabineer and checked three times that it was secure before she started to pull the rope.

The further Billy got from the edge, the more he barked, growled, and struggled. Matilda could see he was trying to chew through the carrier.

Frantically she pulled, and finally the rope stopped moving. She held the walkie-talkie, waiting to hear Lowky's voice.

"Got him!" Lowky said, and they both breathed a sigh of relief.

"On my way" Matilda said as she put the walkie-talkie in her back pocket and headed for the ladder. She had no time to be scared. The rain was getting heavier, the sky was getting darker, and Matilda made it to the other side in half the time it had taken Lowky.

They sat there astonished that they had all made it across without further injuries.

"What now?" Matilda asked anxiously as the rain landed heavily on the supplies. "We should try to bring one of these ladders. It could be very useful."

"Maybe later, but for now let's find some shelter. We're not going anywhere else today," he said as he grabbed his pack. "Maybe we can see from the top of this pile what lies ahead."

They scrambled up the pile, slipping and sliding and falling back to the bottom on several occasions. From the top they could see that the devastation went for miles, but in the distance it appeared that some buildings were standing. Just to the left, about ten metres away, was what looked like the skeleton of a building.

"Over there." Lowky pointed as the rain pelted down around him.

The building was mostly destroyed at the back, and all the windows had been shattered, but one small room at the front offered some protection. They managed to find some dry wood in the mangled mess and stripped to their underwear to dry off. The situation sounds bad, but they were so pumped up that it just added to the adventure. Before long they had dried their clothes (camp clothes are designed to dry very quickly) and were snuggled up in front of the fire. There was no back wall in the room, and it was strangely beautiful watching the rain fall. They drank their coffee and ate baked beans while Billy curled up on Lowky's lap. In fact, after the baby carrier incident, Billy approached Matilda with great caution.

CHAPTER 19

Reunion

THEY woke up without realising they had fallen asleep. The sun was already moving steadily across the sky and the birds had finished their early morning songs. Billy had managed to remove his bandage, which saved Lowky the trouble. The wound was deep and raw and in normal circumstances would have needed stitches, but these were not normal circumstances. Lowky cleaned the wound with as little water as possible. Billy sat patiently but unhappily and squirmed away at the first available opportunity.

Lowky assessed his own injuries and decided they were fine. He felt exhilarated and flashed Matilda a genuine smile as she opened her eyes sleepily.

The supplies were abundant and they all ate breakfast with a healthy and carefree appetite. Lowky had just lifted the steaming coffee pot off the fire when he heard a noise.

"Oh, the smell of coffee, it's the only way to wake an Ecuadorian."

"Oh my God—Marley, Chilli. how did you . . . ? What happened to . . . ? Why . . . ?"

Lowky and Matilda squealed in unison as they jumped up to hug the twins. From the outside it looked like a football team after a tremendous victory. They shrieked and laughed and jumped around like idiots until finally they stood bent over and out of breath.

Billy barked with excitement and they all sat down to share a coffee.

Lowky soon noticed that the twins had packs.

"What's your plan?" he asked curiously, glancing at their supplies.

"We thought we'd come with you," Marley said tentatively. Without saying a word, Chilli looked into Lowky's eyes. He stared with such intensity that Lowky had to look away.

"That would be awesome," Matilda piped in, trying to keep her composure.

"Fantastic." Lowky smiled supportively.

Chilli stood up, his head slightly bowed, and stormed out of the area.

"What's up with him?" Lowky asked, confused.

"He wanted to stay and wait for Dad, but how long can we wait?" she asked as if she expected an answer. "I'm the oldest. I have to do what's best for us."

"What do you mean older, aren't you both 10?" Lowky asked. "Aren't you twins?"

"Yes, but I was born first, a day earlier in fact. I was born at 11:57pm on the 2nd of March and Chilli was born at 12:09am on the 3rd. We have different birthdays and he has always hated it. But the fact is I'm the oldest and I have to make the decisions. Our supplies won't last forever . . ."

"Not the way you Ecuadorians eat," Matilda gently teased.

Marley ignored her and continued. "We can always come back later when things have settled down. I told Chilli we could look for Dad then . . . and we left a note."

Matilda and Lowky nodded silently.

Marley continued. "I wrote how long we'd stayed, what the date was, and where we were going. Then I marked Spargo Creek on a map and left everything in the living room. Then I held it all down with a jar of my dad's favourite pickle, sesame roasted octopus in blood orange butter." She paused, took a breath, closed her eyes, and said, "So can we come with you?"

"Of course, of course." Matilda beamed, answering without hesitation.

"Of course," Lowky added.

Marley smiled wearily and turned around to look for Chilli. She didn't have to look far; he was sitting on the other side of the wall sulking quietly in the rain. It wasn't long before she had convinced him to return.

Lowky put his arm gently on Chilli's shoulder, but he flicked it away as if he had somehow been betrayed. For the rest of the afternoon and for many days to come, Chilli rarely spoke a word, and when he did speak it was only out of necessity.

The arrival of the twins was a small miracle. Lowky and Matilda had forgotten to bring a map and a can opener, both of which the twins had remembered, and both of which were essential.

CHAPTER 20

Plateau

For three days and three nights they climbed, stumbled, tripped, fell, and climbed again. Matilda and Lowky were positive and light. They had already negotiated the initial stages of grief. The twins had not, and they were new to travelling, both now and in their history. They were a decadent family that prided themselves on hard but clean work. Unlike Matilda and Lowky, the twins were used to luxury. This was more than a challenge for them; it was a complete culture shock. Even after the earthquake they had managed to wrap themselves in a cloak of relative normalcy.

They all walked quietly, but Chilli was the quietest as he walked with Billy, who was scouting up ahead.

Billy often stopped to lead the group through any difficult or treacherous terrain. He was a psychic in his own way, knowing when to move, stop, wait, or warn. Chilli took Billy on as his only friend. He clearly felt he had been betrayed by everyone else. They would go wandering in the evening under the guise of finding firewood. Chilli would sit in the rubble out of earshot. He would pat Billy, hug and hold him, crying into his fur. Billy took these walks willingly, sat their patiently, and then returned to the group at the perfect time.

Chilli had initially refused to move. He knew his sister would never leave without him. How Marley got Chilli across the ladders was a sight to behold and a story for another time, but once he was across he sat in the open room around the fire and refused to move again. Lowky tried, Matilda tried, Marley tried, but nothing! Then quietly and without regret, Billy walked over to Chilli, licked his face, sat on his lap, and looked him square in the eyes. This lasted for about five minutes as everyone sat around puzzled by what was happening.

"Come on, Billy, get off, we have to go." Lowky giggled but Billy was steadfast and unwavering in his resolve. Chilli still refused to speak but stared intently back at Billy. Then all of a sudden, without reason, Billy licked Chilli's cheek again, got up, walked behind him, and bit him fair on the bottom. Chilli jumped up with a scream and snapped, "What'd you do that for?" but Billy just looked at him lovingly and then bared his teeth with a fierceness none of them had ever seen. Reluctantly Chilli began to walk, and for a long time Billy stayed apologetically by his side.

Finally, as they climbed another pile of what seemed to be an eternity of rubble, Lowky paused to address them. "This is ridiculous. As you know we only have enough food and water for one more day, and that's if we eat and drink very little. It's time to come up with a plan."

"Let's just get to the top of this pile," Marley said, exhausted. "It's massive, so maybe well be able to see ahead."

"This is the tallest pile so far—it's like a mountain," Lowky agreed.

Of course getting to the top was problematic. Firstly, Chilli and his attitude caused them to take one step forward and two steps back. The pile of rubble was also unique: it was high, really high, and the higher the rise the bigger the threat. There were thousands of loose pieces of stone, cement, glass, and wood that shifted and moved like the lungs of a monster. On top of that, they had to negotiate miles of twisted and buckled steel that trapped their hands and feet like huge spindly fingers. The steel in places had torn and was razor sharp. With every step Lowky could hear the cries of what used to be a strong and beautiful city.

Marley screamed as a jagged piece of wood splinted her hand. "Geez!" she screamed again as she grabbed one end and tried desperately to pull it out. The splinter was enormous; it was about one centimetre wide and thirty centimetres long.

Ouch! Lowky squirmed discreetly as he twisted and slid across the "mountain" to help her.

Billy somehow got to Marley first even though he had already been to the summit and was on his way back down again.

Matilda and Lowky looked at each other in amazement as it was physically impossible, but they shrugged it off to deal with the crisis at hand.

"Okay, Marley, relax for one second and let me have a look." Lowky coaxed but it was too late.

Chilli had also magically appeared from the bottom of the rubble. He was speaking frantically to Marley in Spanish. They both spoke for a few seconds and then something changed. Chilli and Marley both calmed down. With one joined breath they worked methodically. Quietly Chilli went around to the back of her pack and pulled out a small bottle of blood-red liquid. Again he spoke in Spanish, and Marley took two large sips of the liquid. Then Chilli took the bottle and carefully dabbed a small amount at the entrance of the wound. Marley took two more swigs and then waited for the elixir to take effect. About two minutes later Chilli started to talk again. Marley and Chilli both started laughing as Matilda and Lowky looked at each other curiously.

Then, without warning, in English Chilli announced, "One, two . . ."

They all waited tentatively for three, but by the time they realised what had happened, Chilli had removed the splinter and was starting to bandage Marley's hand. It wasn't until Marley saw the blood quickly soak trough the bandage that she finally fainted.

There they stayed, perched like mountain goats, taking turns on avalanche watch.

Nobody knew how Lowky collected the wood and started a fire, but he did. It was small but effective and Chilli and Matilda managed to turn their last can of baked beans, some random dried herbs, and a sachet of tartar sauce into something edible. They hadn't eaten since the night before and they all fidgeted anxiously as the concoction was prepared. It was amazing how little could be turned into a meal. Lowky was going to make some bread, but there was only enough flour for two small loaves, and no one wanted to waste it on Lowky's baking skills. They decided unanimously to wait until Marley was well enough to bake again. This momentarily offended Lowky, but he admitted quietly to himself that he too would prefer Marley's bread.

Things became more difficult now that Marley was injured. Chilli stayed mainly by her side, helping her up as best he could. When it all got too much for him they stopped and Lowky and Matilda split her supplies, which by now was not a very heavy load. Matilda and Chilli stayed with Marley, plodding along slowly as Billy and Lowky went up ahead to set up camp and see what was on offer on the other side. It was mid-morning, and the relentless drizzle of the last three days had finally stopped.

Lowky's excitement grew as he neared the top. With the stops and the split and the devastation, Lowky had completely lost track of how far they'd come or where they were. They were still in the city, but he imagined they were leaving the outer northern suburbs behind them.

As Lowky approached the summit, his heart started to beat with a mighty power. He was both exhausted and exhilarated and held on tight as his hand shakily reached for a stable rock at the top. He was perched on his hands and feet. The hand that wasn't holding the top gripped frantically onto metal as the mountain shifted beneath his feet.

"Heads up!" he yelled as small pieces of stone and cement went tumbling towards the other three. One rather large stone hit Matilda on the back of the head.

Lowky tried desperately to get a good footing to push him to the top, but the more he struggled to kick his leg over, the more loose debris fell towards the others. He looked up to see Billy perched over the edge, trying to grab at the handle of his backpack with his teeth. As Lowky pulled and Billy perched, they were only centimetres apart. Lowky pulled again, his feet thrashing underneath him. Billy barked between thrashes, snipping towards the bag whenever he thought he had a chance. No matter how hard Lowky tried, he couldn't do it and his fingers were starting to give way. He looked up at Billy in defeat. Billy barked vigilantly at Lowky and continued his determined focus on the backpack. Lowky looked up, and with all his might he tried to swing his leg up to the top of the mountain. He was so unsuccessful it was embarrassing, but out of nowhere his pants got caught on a piece of wood. He used the last of his strength to get his knee over and then he hung there, upside down and exhausted, for what seemed like hours.

Finally he moved. His head was spinning, and with his last ounce of energy he hauled himself up and over.

He lay there exhausted and panting. Billy barked triumphantly, and Lowky finally got to look over the edge. He immediately rolled back to where he had just come from, even lower, with no memory of how hard it had been to get there.

He frantically called Billy, but Billy was reluctant to move. In his best "parent voice," Lowky growled, "Billy! Now!"

Billy scampered down the mound to Lowky's feet, and they both sat there breathless and silent until the others arrived.

Lowky had seen something extraordinary. On the other side of the mountain the earth was flat and smooth and the buildings were standing. Well, partially standing. The group later found out that the mountain was not only rubbish from the quake but a collection of rubble from the streets and buildings. Most of the areas Lowky had seen had been cleared and organised.

But that wasn't what made Lowky jump. It was the people. There were lots of them, all going about their daily business. The sun was shining on them, but luckily for Lowky no one was looking up. He knew they were going no further today, so he started to set up camp. For the first time in a long time he decided he didn't need the tarp, not yet anyway. He decided that lighting a fire was also a bad idea. As far as food went they were down to two packets of kangaroo jerky, one packet of tomato soup, and two Snickers bars. Seeing that there was no fire, it would have to be kangaroo jerky for lunch—and yes, it tastes as bad as it sounds.

It took ages for the rest of the group to arrive. Lowky watched as they stumbled up the mountain like a line of rebellious ants. Marley had to stay on her feet as using only one good hand kept her off balance. Matilda and Chilli took turns standing in front of her to pull her up and behind her to catch her when she lost her footing, which was often. Finally they got to Lowky and asked in unison, "Didn't you get to the top? It looked like you got to the top? Can we get to the top?"

Lowky explained all about the clearing and the people.

"Well, so what!" Matilda said, excited. "Why don't we take a peek?"

"It's not that easy. The only way to get to the top is to be at the top and it's near impossible to get there; you can't just peek! If you go to the top you take the risk of being seen," Lowky explained.

"Does it really matter? If it's as organised as you say, we can just say our parents are down the road!"

"Really? We look like hobos and were standing on top of an impossible mountain, I just don't think they'd fall for that." Lowky said.

"Well what do you suggest, Einstein?" she snapped as she dusted off her muddied and bloodied camping clothes. "We have almost no food or water, and from what you say there is clearly food and water down there. We can't go back! So, now what?"

"Well, I've had a chance to think about that," he replied with a smile.

"And?" Matilda softened.

"I think we should walk across the ridge on this side and see if we can find a quieter and easier place to have a good look down. If possible, we should go down at night. We might just blend in if we can find some clothes and clean up a bit. If we travel mainly at night we should be able to replenish some of our supplies. We may even be able to get our hand on some fresh food."

"Yeah, right!" Matilda laughed.

Lowky was about to snap back, but Chilli chimed in. "Maybe someone down there has seen our dad," he said softly.

"Maybe," Lowky said, a little annoyed. "Chilli you can leave whenever you want, but our parents are dead." He looked at Matilda. "And we've made a pact to get to Spargo Creek. We want you to stay, but we won't force you. You and Marley must decide, but if you stay with us we have to make every effort not to get caught."

Lowky looked at Chilli, who was clearly torn. "Look, Chilli, you and Marley can talk about it and decide after lunch. Whatever you decide we'll help you the best we can." He paused. "Come on, we have a delicious delicacy, sought-after all around the world. Yes, it's your lucky day! Dry, chewy, old, stinky, and dead kangaroo!" He handed Chilli a piece and they both laughed.

From where they were, the mountain sort of turned north, so it was hard to see what lay ahead. Chilli and Marley suggested they go and scout things out. There was no point having an impossible plan, plus it gave them a chance to talk. They didn't have to walk long until they were out of sight.

"It looks possible," Marley started, as she had decided to try and convince Chilli to stay with the others. Once they settled down in Spargo Creek, if their dad was alive they would find him.

"I want to go with Lowky and Matilda, but I will never leave you, Chilli. I believe if Dad is alive we'll find him, but now is not the time. How can we find him down there in this state? Please, Chilli, let's go with them. They're all we've got!"

"Okay . . ." Chilli said quietly but Marley interrupted.

"I know you're scared, but if Dad's out there, I promise you we'll find him."

"I said okay."

"I know, but I really think if we go down there now . . ."

This time Chilli interrupted. "Marley!" he shouted. "I said okay." Chilli was so loud that Lowky and Matilda heard him and flashed each other a smile.

Marley threw her arms around him and hugged him till he squealed with a pretend dislike.

"I love you, Chilli," she said, and she meant it.

"I know." He giggled as she tried to chase him back around the corner to the others.

"So you're staying?" Matilda confirmed.

"Yep, for now."

CHAPTER 21

—◦—

People

A s they negotiated the ridge, before the peak they began to get excited about normalcy. Not the "meat and three veg" type of normalcy; no, it was more the little things. Matilda heard a bird sing and was embarrassed but overjoyed by the fact that it made her cry.

"Did you hear that?" Lowky squealed, and they all stopped with excitement to hear the next sound. "Shhh, I think it's someone talking."

"They must be yelling for us to be able to hear it."

"Shhh, Matilda, just wait . . ." Lowky said.

They all fell into a deep silence, and within a few seconds the sound started again. "Yes, its definitely voices," Matilda said.

They all looked at each other and started to walk again, this time with more purpose and determination.

"I can't wait to get down there!" Marley smiled. "Tell us again what it's like, Lowky."

Lowky told them all he knew and a bit he wished he had seen. It was almost nighttime when the ridge they had been travelling on started to slope upward towards the peak of the mountain.

"This is it," Matilda said in anticipation, "this is the closest we've been."

"Let's go to the peak now," Marley added.

They all wanted to look over the edge before it was too dark to see anything. Getting to the peak at that point wasn't that hard, but they could only do it one at a time. They decided Lowky would go last, which meant Matilda would be the first person to have a really good look at the plateau.

Matilda was overwhelmed. Lowky was right; it was like another world. People were walking around or gathered in groups, talking. There was a road that got smoother the further it got away from the mountain. Some people had put sheets or whatever they could find out on the road and were selling things. Matilda couldn't make out what was being sold, but it was a popular area and many people mingled around.

It was not an area where they would be able to descend the mountain. She looked further to the left, where some buildings were still standing. The area had been cleared, but the roads were damaged and crumbling. She could see one sizable split in the earth, which she followed with her eyes further to the left. As she looked, the split got larger and larger until it opened its mouth into a giant abyss, even bigger than the split they had crossed with the ladders. Between the market and the abyss would be the best place to enter. There were fewer people, and in some areas there were no people at all.

Matilda could have stayed up there forever, exploring with her eyes, but she wanted to let the others see. She wanted to make a plan before it got dark. She wanted to hear voices, see faces; she wanted to smell things other than old dust and death.

Marley was the next to go up. Chilli never did anything Marley hadn't tested first. Marley saw everything Matilda had seen, but she didn't absorb it in the same way. Matilda had looked at it like an adventurer, a survivor about to conquer the last frontier before the *Promised Land*.

Marley looked at it like a reminder of what they had lost; a reminder that nothing would ever be the same again. She came down crying and could not remember any detail of what she had seen. Chilli would not go up after that, so it was finally Lowky's turn. He anxiously followed the path to the summit, happily looking for hope ahead.

Lowky and Billy climbed the small peak to the top. He had heard Matilda's excitement and was smiling even before he got there. He tried not to think of the Sal-Hencos on the way up. He tried to stay positive on the edge of his fear.

Lowky saw what Matilda had seen and more. The people from the market, the road, and the edges of the abyss were all gathering and starting to walk in one direction. Unseen people came from under awnings and behind obstructions and all gathered in a mass that moved like a cancer through the veins of a very sick city. They headed away from the mountain, and Lowky watched frozen as the mass slid north along the smooth road and completely out of sight.

Marley had stopped crying and was sharing notes with Matilda when Lowky and Billy returned. Matilda had sketched the scene in her black book, and Lowky added to the drawing as he tried to explain the mass exodus that had occurred.

"Well, we have no choice; we have to go down there eventually."

"Eventually!" Lowky said. "I don't know what you plan on eating tonight, and we've been out of water since lunch. We have to go tonight while we still have the energy."

"Did you notice any lights?" Chilli asked.

"No, but it's not dark yet," Lowky said.

"Well, it's too dark," Chilli snapped, "and we need good light to get to the bottom. I haven't come this far to go all Humpty Dumpty down the side."

"I swear everyone left, and if some people did stay there sure aren't many of them. We have to go tonight," Lowky said. "It's our only chance to get supplies."

"We ain't gonna find them up here, that's for sure," Matilda said. "I'm with you, Lowky—we go tonight."

"If there are no people," Marley started, "and you said that they packed up all their things, then there will be no supplies, right? We should just go at dawn before the people come back, if they come back."

"If the mass don't come back." Lowky said, "they will have to sleep somewhere, and if we go tonight at least we're closer to catching up with them."

"Whatever we do, we have to decide now! Chilli's right—it's getting dark quickly, and if we go down we need to do it immediately. Let's vote. All in favour of going down tonight raise your hand," Marley said.

Lowky and Matilda raised their hands.

"It's a draw," Lowky said, disappointed. "What now?"

They sat there silently for a second until Matilda stood up and started to put her pack on. "We'll split up! Lowky, Billy, and I will go down tonight."

Lowky looked at her curiously.

"It'll be easier if it's just two of us anyway. At least if we can find some food and water for tomorrow, it's a start," she said.

"I'm in," Lowky said. "You guys can come down at dawn, and hopefully we'll have some clothes for you."

Marley loved the plan and was more than willing to hold back even without water. Her hand was still in pain, and she had no desire to struggle tonight.

"We'll be able to form a proper plan in the morning after we're down there and have a clearer view," Chilli added.

"Come to the peak with me, Marley" Matilda said. She was ready to go. "We can pick a meeting point while Lowky and Chilli pack up."

Marley and Matilda scouted out a spot for them to meet. It was the only bit of colour they could find: a red streak in the landscape, about twenty metres from the market.

By the time Marley came back down, Lowky and Billy were ready to go. The only food Lowky could leave for the twins was the half jar of pickles Matilda had hidden in her pack on the first day at the hardware store. Lowky took the flour, as it was useless without water. They packed up everything the twins couldn't use. It was heavy, but with Marley's injured hand she couldn't carry anything.

"You've been good to us, Lowky." Marley smiled as Lowky started to move towards the peak.

"We're in this together." He smiled shyly as he tapped his leg and moved over so Billy could run ahead. "See you soon," he called as he disappeared out of sight.

Lowky met Matilda on the peak. He beamed at her, and as they started to descend the dangerous slope, fear was washed away with excitement. They talked all the way down about the whys and what ifs and before they knew it their feet touched smoothness for the first time since the crossing.

They looked around with great anticipation, their eyes and ears on full alert. They saw nothing. Lowky shuffled through his pack for two torches and a spotlight, which he attached to Billy's collar.

"Wait," Matilda whispered. "Turn it off."

Lowky fumbled with the button.

"Quick, Lowky, quick!" and with that they were in near darkness again. The sun had long gone but there was still a remainder of it across the sky. Lowky and Billy looked at Matilda intently as they waited for her to explain.

"I heard something, voices I think." They all sat there listening, and before long they heard the sound of voices. It seemed like a small group.

"Let's get closer and try to hear what their saying," Lowky whispered, and the three of them quietly through the night. They could just make out the ground ahead, and their hearts started to pound as the voices got louder and a light appeared.

"You have to make up your mind by tomorrow, Jimmy. This is craziness. We need to put our name on the list," a gentle and patient female voice said.

"I'm telling you, Joan, you're crazy if you think we're better off with them. Finding food for us is hard enough. I heard they had dropped crates of food to the north."

"There's safety in numbers," another female said in great frustration. "We have probably already missed our opportunity."

"What opportunity?" asked another.

"He's right you know," added a new male voice. "We can't even feed ourselves—how is what we find going to be spread between hundreds?"

"We have nothing, and we have to get to the mainland. Do you really think we can do it alone?" This was more of a joke than a question, and the group went quiet until the first man spoke again.

"Look, if we go to the water tanks tonight, we can stock up before everyone comes back tomorrow."

"What if they don't come back?"

"You heard them all in the market today, didn't you? They're holding one more day of trading, and then they're all moving east the day after tomorrow."

Lowky and Matilda had counted five different voices, two men and three women. The window of the building that the strangers had been sitting in had been shattered in the earthquake and the pair could see the flicker of candlelight coat the dusty walls.

"We still have things to trade—maybe we can trade for food at the market tomorrow," Joan interrupted.

"No one's trading food, Jimmy; you know that."

"I know, but I have seeds, and surely an abundance of food later is better than a small amount now."

"You really are crazy," the second female said. "How can we survive alone? We must register tomorrow and go east with the others. Food drops in the north are just rumours—and where north? How far? It's impossible, Jimmy, impossible"

"What do you think, Abdi?"

"I think you should do what you want! We're connected by nothing except time, and that, as intense as it has been, is, in fact, very little." He paused to clear his throat. "I'm going north, with or without any of you. Our meeting has been remarkable, but I am not for crowds or control. I will not travel with the pack."

There was clearly no reason for them to stay together.

"Well." Jimmy piped up again. "Tonight is obviously for thinking, so we can decide in the morning. The pack won't be back before seven. I have some biscuits and a can of fruit juice." The kids heard him fumble through his pack and place something, likely his supplies, in the pile.

"I have an egg and a lighter," Abdi added.

"Two potatoes," another added.

"Three cans of spaghetti, pancake mix, jam, honey . . ."

"What? How?" They all asked. Even Lowky and Matilda, who were now moving away from the window, stopped in their tracks to hear the woman's explanation.

"I've been doing a lot of walking near the wall," she said.

Lowky elbowed Matilda and whispered, "The mountain. It's the only area this side of the earthquake that hasn't been cleared."

"And?" Jimmy pushed as he watched her still pulling supplies out of her backpack.

"Well, yesterday I found a little tunnel that went directly into the very foundations of the mountain. I managed to squeeze through. I had to crawl about three metres, and then it seemed to open up into a huge cave. It was pitch dark, so I decided to take my torch with me this morning as soon as the sun came up."

"And?" Jimmy repeated as they all sat transfixed, mouths open, breathing stopped.

"Well, you would never guess it. I found what I think is an old arcade. The opening I came to yesterday was actually a corridor that stands for about fifteen metres and then crumbles into the wall. On both sides of the corridor two shops have remained. The shops are standing at the entrance and then crumbling about a third of the way in."

Everyone stayed still and stared at the woman.

She continued. "One of the shops, the one in the best condition, is a mini-mart. I just sat on the floor and ate. I don't know for how long, but it was a long time. Then I filled up my pack and brought it here."

She was digging at the bottom of her bag for the last of the goods when Abdi finally broke the silence. "Is there any more food, Joan?" he asked.

"Heaps." She smiled warmly. "More than we could ever carry."

"What were the other stores?" Jimmy asked hopefully.

"Umm, jeans, chemist, two-dollar shop, oh, and a tiny section of a sports store. I managed to find this"—she smiled as she unclipped a baseball cap from her pack and pulled her filthy ponytail through the hole in the back.

"We must go now," Jimmy piped up. "We must get as many loads as we can before morning."

"We have more than enough for tonight, trust me—nobody knows it's there. Everyone has given up on the wall; no one is looking back. It's unstable and dangerous. We can all go in tomorrow morning, one at a time."

"Why can't—" Jimmy interrupted.

"No! Let me finish," Joan said forcefully. "I have been thinking about this all day. We go first thing in the morning. Everyone goes in one at a time and fills his or her packs with whatever each person needs. I have decided I am going north with Abdi and anyone else who wants to come. Once we have collected everything we need, I will tell someone about the corridor so the others can clean it out before they go."

The woman took a breath. "Jimmy's right. No matter what decision you make, if we all get up early, at least we can stock up for the journeys that lie ahead."

"Agreed," Abdi said as he curled up on the jacked he had been using as a bed.

"Agreed," Joan, who had already said she would not be going north, added.

"Agreed," Jimmy said.

*

Lowky, Matilda, and Billy moved quickly as one by one the candles were blown out and they realized they were now in complete darkness. Matilda silently found her small reading torch and together they walked effortlessly on the cleared, even road. When they were far enough away, they turned on both of the large torches and started looking for a place to base themselves.

Matilda said, "We need to stay away from the market." She paused. "The closer we get to the abyss, the safer we'll be."

Lowky agreed, and they turned right at the next possible intersection. The further they got from the centre of the plateau, the more they stumbled. The earth started to separate and rise, and eventually, nothing stable remained. They stopped walking and looked back towards the market.

"Let's try that building," Matilda said as she pointed to a solid wall just to the left of them.

They approached the room tentatively. The roof had detached and was leaning diagonally against the southern wall. Sections of the rafters and plaster had fallen into the room, but there was still a large area that was covered and out of view from the street. The floor at the back had collapsed under the weight of the relentless rain; however, the sun that had shined over the last two days had significantly dried it out. They decided it would make an adequate and safe camping site for what appeared would be a minimum two-night stay.

"We have to go tonight, Lowky."

"Where exactly?" he asked, exhausted.

"To the arcade and the water tanks."

"Are you crazy? No way! We'll go tomorrow with the twins."

"No, think about it. We can get food, clothes, and water all before the mass come back, and once we meet the twins we'll be free to look around."

Lowky looked at her in disbelief. "Do you really think we can do all that tomorrow in the sunlight, looking like this? We have one day, Lowky, and I'll be damned if I'm going to miss the opportunity to go shopping."

He reluctantly agreed and started to set up his bed while Matilda emptied the packs. They had one small and one large pack each. Matilda tied her red T-shirt to a piece of cement outside to use as a marker.

"We should start at the beginning of the mountain," he suggested. "That way, we hopefully won't miss the entrance."

"But we'll be in the middle, so I'm guessing the water tanks are somewhere near the market." Matilda looked at Lowky sternly. "I need some water."

"Okay, Matilda, you're right. The twins will be desperate by the time they get to the meeting point. We'll just have to do the mountain in two parts."

They walked silently side by side. The group they had encountered earlier was probably not the only people lurking behind.

Everything looked different in the dark, and as the marketplace had been stripped bare it was hard to identify. They came to a very smooth, very clean, almost flat street.

"This must be it," Lowky whispered. "You check the front and I'll search at the back." He looked around with a cheeky grin. "We'll meet back here."

"No way," Matilda growled. "We stay together. Anything could happen. We'll search the front first."

"Okay, then. Let's go, Billy," Lowky said as they headed towards the street just east of the market.

"Where's Billy?" Matilda said as they both looked around frantically.

"Billy, Billy Baxter!" they screamed in their loudest whisper. Lowky's heart was in his chest as he searched through his bag for a bigger torch.

"Billy Baxter," Matilda repeated in a relieved tone and Lowky looked up to see him coming around the side of a building. He walked up to Matilda, who patted him lovingly.

"Hey, his mouth's wet," she accidentally squealed.

"You cheeky bugger," Lowky whispered to himself. "Come on, Billy, show us the water!"

Billy looked at him with what Lowky swore was a smile, and then off he trotted back the way he came.

"It can't be far," Lowky whispered to Matilda, and then suddenly Billy came to a complete stop. They did the same. Billy crept forward as if on tiptoes. They followed. Billy got to a sharp corner and stopped again. They could see a flickering light and stopped and waited to see Billy's next move. He waited. They moved a little closer, curiosity getting the better of them. Billy just waited. They moved a little closer, but Billy growled his quietest growl and they stepped back. Billy looked at them angrily, teeth exposed, and then slinked around the corner.

Lowky and Matilda were too scared to move so they waited, frozen, for Billy to return. He did, and again Lowky swore the dog was smiling. He brushed lightly across them both and then headed back around the corner with a confident stride. They followed. The second they got around the corner they froze again. The light had been coming from a fire that was starting to die out.

A man and a woman were sitting on crates in front of the fire, leaning against a wall. Both were fast asleep, heads tilted forward.

Lowky looked around for Billy but was blown away by the sight to his left: water tanks, not one or two but about twenty. He nudged Matilda, who was still staring at the sleeping guards.

"Oh my God, Lowky," Matilda whispered, "where's Billy now?" They looked around to see him drinking silently from a puddle.

Lowky's mouth salivated, and before long he was down on his knees scooping water from Billy's puddle. Matilda followed.

"We need a plan," Lowky said, water dripping from his chin.

"Let's go back," Matilda suggested, "just for a minute." Once they were out of hearing range they breathed a joint sigh of relief.

"This is our only chance of getting to that water," Lowky huffed. "Once the mass is back . . ."

"Maybe we can pretend to be part of the mass! If we try and turn on one of those tanks, we'll wake those guards for sure!"

"Come on, Matilda, we have to try. Remember those people said something about having to register. What would we do then, and what about the twins? They won't be able to wait another day. We have to try something."

"No way, it's too dangerous. How on earth?"

"Well." Lowky paused, searching for a plan. His eyes darted about in the near darkness, as if searching for a clue.

Billy was waiting patiently. "We'll put Billy on guard!" he stated without anything to back it up. "And . . . we'll be as quiet as we can."

Matilda looked at him smugly.

"Oh, you come up with a better plan," he snapped.

"Okay, it's not a bad start. Billy, can you growl?" she whispered but he just looked at her. "Billy, growl!" Billy smiled. Lowky laughed. "What?" Matilda snapped.

"Didn't you see Billy smile?" Lowky asked, giggling.

"What?" Matilda repeated with faked patience.

"Oh forget it." Lowky sighed as he waited for her to continue.

"I think Billy will growl if they wake up. We can at least try and get as much water as possible until then! If they wake up, we split up and meet back at the base?"

"Okay." Lowky smiled. It had been his idea, after all!

Once they got back to the tanks, they split up. Lowky went to the closet row while Matilda went two rows back. Billy had immediately walked to the guards without having to be asked. Lowky approached a tank and pulled the large faucet as slowly and quietly as possible. It creaked loudly, and one of the guards shuffled on his create.

Billy was ready to pounce, teeth exposed, not a sound—but the man fell back asleep unawares. Nothing happened, so Lowky pulled the handle around a little further; still nothing.

He went to the next tank. The handle was different from the first, and he struggled to move it. When he finally did, it moved quickly, letting out a large scraping sound. He waited as the adrenalin pulsed through his body. His head spun and he had to steady himself against the side of the tank. He pulled once more at the faucet, but no water came out. *There's no water,* Lowky thought desperately.

He started to walk forward, looking for Matilda. He could see her legs from under the tanks. She was also rushing from tank to tank, making not a single sound. She held a plastic bottle in her hand, and at each tank it remained empty.

There's no water, Lowky repeated to himself, each time more defeated than the time before. He was about to go back when he heard that voice, soft and sweet, say, *Keep looking.*

Lowky got up and went to the next tank. He was now in the second row. It was a small tank, and he knew if he could knock on the side he would know whether it had water in it. It was too risky, so he turned the faucet and held his breath. Nothing. He tried another and then another.

He was just about to give up—again—when he thought about it logically. *If the tanks were empty, they wouldn't have guards. They must be running out of water and that's why they're leaving.*

Lowky looked over at Billy and the guards. They were placed in a very odd position; they were in the front row but way over to the left-hand side. Lowky quietly moved to the tanks behind the guards. He was about three rows back when he tried his next faucet—again nothing. He moved into the second row and turned the closest tap he could find. It bubbled loudly, and again the male guard shifted in his seat.

With Billy on guard, Lowky screamed a silent cheer as water started splashing noisily to the ground. Matilda must have heard the noise because she came running over and placed her bottle under the flow. Once Matilda's bottle was full, Lowky placed his under the tap. This continued until they had filled every last container, and both the small and large backpacks were full to the brim. Lowky leaned over to turn off the tap, but this time it bubbled and scraped as it ground itself shut. The female guard jumped to her feet. Lowky and Matilda swung on the backpacks as Billy waited, ready to attack.

"Come, Billy," Lowky whispered. "Quietly, Billy, come!"

Billy started walking backward, teeth bared, eyes on the target. He reached Lowky before the woman had a chance to focus properly, and they all started retreating backward through the dark.

"Oh, Susan, what's up?" the man said sleepily.

"I thought I heard something. I thought I saw something."

"I don't see anything," he said as he stretched and yawned dismissively.

"I'm sure . . ." Her voice trailed off as she sat back on her crate and stoked the fire.

By this time, Lowky, Matilda, and Billy had retreated back into the shadows, and it wasn't long before they were making their first drop off at base.

CHAPTER 22

Arcade

THEY had been searching the mountain for hours. There were so many tunnels to search as almost every step revealed a new opening. First Matilda crawled in to see if they led to anything, but the going was tough and the disappointment was oppressive. Lowky took over the crawling while Matilda held the torch and stood guard. Every dead end was exhausting, and eventually they had no choice but to trust Billy with the job. He did this effortlessly, but they had no idea if he knew what he was looking for.

The trio were now almost at the very east end of the mountain when Billy came out and barked.

"Are you sure, Billy?" Matilda said as she started to approach the entrance. Billy sat down and wagged his tail.

Matilda went first and Lowky followed. Once they had crawled their way through the first section the mouth widened, and before they knew it they were standing comfortably side by side.

It was exactly like the woman had described. The supermarket was on the right, and without a word they both walked in and picked up the closest edible thing. Lowky opened a can of braised steak and onion for Billy and then grabbed a can of baked beans for himself. He thought back to that first day in his destroyed house and he wished just for a second that he could rewind the memory back to when he was sitting around the TV with his mum and sister. Everything they had encountered had distracted him until now, but a wall of fear hit him hard in the chest. He replaced the baked beans and grabbed a can of fruit salad instead. He didn't want to talk, which was good because Matilda was too busy stuffing her face with a muesli bar.

"Thank God for that!" Matilda mumbled as she shoved the last of a second bar into her mouth."

Lowky didn't say anything.

"We need to move fast. We'll grab food this trip and all the rest in the next trip. Those people will be here at dawn, maybe before," Matilda suggested, but Lowky was already filling his backpack with food.

The supermarket was medium size, and although it was completely destroyed at the back, large amounts of canned and packet goods were sprawled everywhere, more than enough for them and the adults and about ten other people too. This time there was no dog food. Lowky collected anything with meat in it for Billy: Spam, pâté , spaghetti and meatballs. He tried to find packet stuff for everyone else as it was lighter and easier to carry.

"Can't we just do one trip?" he mumbled.

"What about the twins? They need supplies and they have plenty of room in their packs."

"Yeah, but we've already collected four bags of water, and we have to split that too."

"We'll be here at least two days, and we want to be as loaded as possible."

"We'll find a bag and carry two days' supply in that."

"All right already! Food in the big packs and everything else in the small ones. I'll collect the supplies for the next two days, but you're carrying them," Matilda teased.

"I'll get two bags," Lowky said, trying to smile as he walked out of the supermarket. Directly in front of him was the jeans shop. It was the same as the supermarket, relatively undamaged at the front, non-existent at the back. A table stood in the middle of the entrance, its contents mainly on the floor. One broken leg meant that some items had pooled in the front corner, and Lowky picked them up one by one. He pulled out two T-shirts—one for him and one for Chilli. They were a thick material with a Hawaiian design printed across the front. He also found a T-shirt with a four leaf clover, which he kept for himself. At the left he found men's jeans, but they were huge so he passed them and found some three-quarter pants. Lowky immediately got undressed. His clothes were revolting. Up until two days ago they had had enough water to wash their undies, but everything else hadn't been cleaned since they left the hardware store, and for a while now they had stunk. Lowky found no undies, so he put the pants on over his old ones. They were huge, they were long in the leg, and the waist was massive. He tried another pair and another. Yep, he still hated shopping. Finally he found a pair of shorts, and with the aid of a belt he managed to make them fit. He grabbed both of these items for Chilli. He didn't dare choose for Matilda, so she left her to pick for the girls. On the left were a few pairs of oversized shoes, and then the shop became the mountain.

Lowky came back on the opposite side carrying two long-sleeve tops, two one-piece wrestling singlets, four pairs of socks, and four plastic bags.

"Don't you look suave?" Matilda said as he walked back into the supermarket.

"You go get some stuff for you and Marley, and I'll finish up here."

"I've filled the packs. You just need to get the supplies for the plastic bags," she said as she walked out the door.

Lowky had almost filled the last bag when Matilda walked back through the door. She had changed and was almost unrecognisable. Lowky smiled as he loaded and stuffed in two bottled waters and looked at Matilda.

"You said get supplies for the next two days. We don't want to waste our travelling water," he said as he tried to squeeze another one in. "Plus," he said with a grin, "I'm going to have a bath."

It was very late by the time they got back to base. Lowky started the fire he had prepared earlier and within seconds they were lying on their jacket beds fast asleep.

CHAPTER 23

Late

MATILDA jumped out of bed, startled. The fire had completely burnt out, and somehow Lowky was still sleeping.

"Oh my God, Lowky, I heard something," she squealed. "Lots of something . . . oh my God, voices." Matilda kept talking as she shook Lowky out of his dream. "Lowky they're coming this way, they know . . ." Her voice trailed off as if she had remembered something.

Lowky rubbed his eyes and then jumped to his feet. "Matilda, its daytime, the twins—"

Lowky and Matilda had slept through pre-dawn, dawn, early, and mid-morning, and the plateau was buzzing with activity. Their street was far from the action, but they could still hear several groups of people nearby.

"We have to go find them," he said. "I'll grab a pack; let's go!"

They walked out of the base as if they lived there. Lowky chatted confidently to Matilda and they both tried to add some of the things they had heard the night before.

"We must sign up" Matilda said, starting the charade.

"We will today, no one's leaving till tomorrow. Mum said we had till four." They both looked around, but no one had noticed them.

The crowds were like worker bees, busy and focused on the possibility of nectar, working together for a common goal. Lowky noticed no one was smiling, and for a moment he felt guilty that he had smiled so soon. Matilda beamed at him.

"This is awesome, Lowky, let's go to the market."

"Twins first, Matilda. Where did you and Marley decide to meet?"

"Under the streak of red!" She paused, shocked, "Oh God, Lowky! We must be under the streak of red. We won't be able to see it from here."

"Do you remember the area at least?" he asked grumpily. He of course would have picked a more tangible place.

"From the top of the mountain, it was just right of the market." Matilda paused. Her eyes rolled towards the sky as she fell deep into thought. "It wouldn't be too far from the arcade."

"Okay. Well, let's just get there. We can try and get a higher vantage point from closer to the mark, but we're late. Let's go."

"Who made you king of the world, Mr. Tick? You would still be asleep now if it wasn't for me!"

Lowky wasn't willing to justify that with an answer, so he looked at her bitterly and started walking towards the market. This time Billy stayed with Matilda, at least until she started to follow.

Everything looked different in the light. It smelt different too. There was an overwhelming combination of hot bread and coffee with and under-scent of porridge and—

"Oh my God, is that basil?" Lowky stammered as he made a sharp left turn and started heading towards the smell. Memories flooded back: his mum in their garden pulling out the old basil and lovingly collecting the seeds. There was also Spargo Creek and Ales making toasties, not to mention Aunt Edie coming over to trade a Vietnamese mint plant for one of his mum's basil plants. The memories continued, and it was as if every encounter Lowky had ever had with basil flashed before his eyes. The smell got stronger, and before long the three of them were standing at the northernmost end of the market, as far from the mountain as the market stretched.

The basil was minimal compared to the intense smell, and from where they were standing it seemed to be the only fresh food. A beaten but happy woman sat cross-legged on the floor behind three potted basil plants as the line in front of her continued to grow. She bartered all kinds of things for just a leaf or two. The next man in line was holding a well-worn pair of walking boots. The woman measured them against her own feet and then asked the man how much.

"Fifteen leaves," he offered confidently.

"Sorry, mate, I have a five-leaf limit." She smiled warmly.

"Five leaves for the boots?" he replied, pretending to be surprised. "It's hardly a fair deal."

"Five leaves is the limit" she replied sternly. He handed her the boots, which she warmly exchanged. The man pretended he was disappointed, but as he turned away Lowky saw a smile spread widely across his face.

"Come on, Lowky, we have to find the twins. Plus we didn't bring anything to trade."

"Okay," he said, the hope of basil washing his grumpiness away. "But later we come to market with supplies and we shop."

As they continued to walk down the main street, they were amazed at the variety of goods for sale: saucepans, clothing, batteries, torches, petrol, and some rare, un-shattered paraphernalia. The group from the night before had been right: apart from the basil lady, no one was selling or trading food. Even so, the crowd was intense as everyone prepared for the big move.

The market stopped about sixty metres from the mountain as the ground became broken and unruly. This was where they turned left. Matilda imagined the red flash to be straight ahead, about the same distance from the mountain as the end of the market.

They walked for another hundred metres before Matilda suddenly stopped and said, "It must be here somewhere." The only vantage point anywhere near them was the water tanks, so they headed towards them.

There was a crowd of people around the four tanks at the back. "Those must be the only ones with water," Lowky pointed. "Won't last long."

They sneaked around to the front trying to go unnoticed and Matilda found an empty tank with a rusty but functional ladder. She climbed to the platform and looked back towards the mountain. It was no use! The remaining buildings blocked her view. She saw another tank even closer to the crowd with a ladder going all the way to the top. It was damaged on one side, but she was sure she could climb it. She went back to the bottom and saw Lowky also trying to conquer a tank.

She moved closer to the other tank and attempted to pull herself up onto the platform. The ladder for this section was missing, and she smiled quietly as she hung monkey-like from the metal structure. She stopped smiling when she landed on her head.

Unperturbed she tried again and again. On her fourth attempt she managed to claw her way to the top of the platform, breathless.

"Hey, what you doing?" a voice called as a hundred faces turned to look at her. She froze for a moment, unable to speak. Finally she managed to glance towards Lowky, who was also looking at her.

"I'm looking for a friend. My phone's not working," she said sarcastically.

He smiled. "How'd you get up there?"

"Magic," she replied, trying to get rid of him.

"You coming tomorrow?" he asked. Matilda glanced at Lowky, who was now well-hidden.

"Of course—isn't everyone?"

"Not everyone!"

"Are you?" she queried as she watched the crowd of faces turn back towards their own activities.

"Where'd you get those jeans" he said, intentionally not answering the question. His own jeans were ripped and dirty.

"The market," she answered casually.

"How much?"

"Five basil leaves."

"Okay, good luck," he said softly as he filled his water bottle and walked away.

"That was close," she whispered to herself as she ran the back of her hand across her forehead.

Lowky watched and smiled.

She turned around to try and find the ladder to the top of the tank. It was on the other side, and soon she was out of sight. She reached for a rung but the ladder creaked as she pulled. With nothing but hope she lifted one foot onto the bottom rung and stood tiptoed on the other. She lifted her other leg, perched fearfully on the side. The ladder screeched and shifted but held dangerously.

When Matilda finally got to the top, she shifted her weight so that her hands were on the tank and her feet were on one of the top rungs. The mountain was huge, even from this height, and she was relieved to see the red streak only about fifty metres away. It was the twisted red roof of a small building they had just walked past. Matilda wondered why the twins hadn't spotted them.

Before heading back down, she looked for a lower landmark and saw a man who appeared to be packing a wheelbarrow. Matilda could only hope he didn't move. She searched anxiously for something more reliable, but everything damaged had been cleared or was covered by the canopies of the last remaining trees.

Matilda shimmied back down the rungs of the ladder with her feet until she was low enough to grab on with her hands. Crack! The whole left bracket snapped and the ladder swung out as if on a hinge. Matilda's back violently hit the tank as she struggled to hold on. She was winded and she choked as she tried to catch her breath. Very slowly she swung the ladder back out and tried to move down another rung. The ledge at the bottom of the tank was very slim and she was too high to jump. She swung back towards the tank, descended one rung, and slammed back again, squashed and trapped. The ladder snapped, crackled, and popped with every step, and Matilda almost chuckled with the sheer absurdity of it.

This continued painfully slowly for the next nine rungs, until Matilda finally stepped onto the platform, bruised and annoyed. For just a second she had forgotten that she still had to get from the platform to the ground, which was supposed to be the difficult part. *It's never-ending* she thought. *Just one obstacle after the other.* Reluctantly she half swung, half fell to the ground, landing only to look up and see Lowky's beaming face.

"You're awesome," he said and immediately continued talking. "Look what I got!" He grinned as he pulled a malachite crystal out of his pocket and showed it to her.

"It's just like the one your mum gave you."

"Sure is, Matilda." He smiled even larger. "It's a sign, Matilda. It's a sign."

Matilda wanted to ask, *A sign of what?* but she didn't have the heart to ruin his moment. She smiled, trying to pretend she was happy for him.

He looked oddly at her. "You know what you need?" "What?" She sighed.

"Some fun. Let's grab the twins and make the most of all these people!"

*

Grabbing the twins proved to be harder than it sounded. They just weren't there. Under the awning with the red streak was a woman selling black tea and coffee, which only made the waiting worse. They had nothing to trade.

Finally, a dishevelled Marley came sulking around the corner. Her hair hung rebelliously in front of her face in big, loose, greasy curls. Her skin was smudged and her clothes no longer showed the pride of an Ecuadorian.

"Marley! Here!" Lowky shouted, feeling much more comfortable around the strangers. She looked at him vaguely and then started giggling as if she had just had laughing gas. She stopped abruptly and just looked at them.

Lowky walked out into the open and pulled her back into the crevasse they had been resting in. "Here, have some water," Lowky said kindly.

She downed the whole bottle and then sat smiling.

"Where's Chilli?" Lowky asked.

Marley's expression immediately changed. "I lost him. I left him here while I tried to find water. When I came back, he was gone." She looked angrily at them both. "This is your fault! Where were you? Some friends!"

They told Marley everything but she just sat silently, absorbing nothing. Finally she looked at them and said, "You were supposed to be here. We would have been better off without you!" As weak as she was she managed to stand up and walk away.

Matilda stood up to follow her. "I'll go help her find him and you stay here in case he comes back."

"Get something to trade," Lowky shouted behind her, but she was already gone.

CHAPTER 24

Lost

MARLEY looked ridiculously out of place in her frantic but exhausted state. Her damaged hand was seeping pus through the bandage, and Matilda was desperate to get her out of sight.

"Let's go back to the base, Marley," she coaxed. "There's food and water and clothes. I'll go look for Chilli in the area behind camp and then come and get you as soon as you've had time to eat and change."

Marley ignored her but followed as her eyes darted back and forth across the terrain. Before long they were back at the camp, but Marley just continued walking.

Matilda ran inside and got a chocolate bar and a bottle of water. She ran back to Marley and waved the water bottle in front of her face. It worked; as Marley reached for it, Matilda took three steps back towards the base. Marley followed momentarily but then stopped dead in her tracks. Matilda handed her the bottle, which she finished immediately. As soon as she stopped drinking, Matilda showed her the chocolate bar and then headed toward the camp.

"The food's all in here," she called back to Marley. Matilda crossed her fingers as she walked through the entrance.

Luckily Marley followed and helped herself to the closest available food, a packet of jelly snakes.

Matilda organised a bowl of water for washing and laid out the clothes she had grabbed at the arcade. "Please, Marley, stay here," she begged. "I won't be long. If I haven't found him, I'll come back, I promise."

Marley said nothing but looked at Matilda with such a cold contempt that Matilda felt she should leave immediately.

"Please, Marley, don't leave without me. I don't want to get anymore lost than we already are."

The second Matilda was out of sight, Marley downed a cold black coffee Lowky had left from the night before. Within five minutes, Marley had eaten, washed, packed some water and food for Chilli, and was back out the door.

Matilda had not even had a chance to check the first street when she saw Marley heading back to the market.

Matilda just stood there, horrified. "*Never split up,*" she thought. *We can't even get that right. This is bullshit,* she hissed as her trademark smile faded to a thickset frown. *We're just kids; really, we should all go with that group.*

She stopped and looked at the sky. *I'm going with the group!* she decided dramatically. *When did that guy say we had to sign up?* Again she looked to the sky. *Sign up for what?*

Matilda's internal voice continued on, relentlessly flooding her with alternative waves of fear and hope, repeating itself like a vacuum salesman as she angrily checked the back streets as she had promised.

The back streets were really starting to fill up with people, lots of people—everyone except Chilli, it seemed. Matilda listened carefully to passing conversations as she discreetly looked behind walls and under awnings. From what Matilda overheard, the most popular items at the market were things for carrying: bikes, backpacks, homemade sleds, and even big bits of cardboard were being traded with great vigour. Rope and coffee were also popular. No food except the basil had been sold that day, and that run out within fifteen minutes. The market would be open till nightfall, and then everyone was to meet at the stadium for the final update before the dawn departure.

Matilda took a deep breath. She hadn't been as excited about a plan since they had left Pyjama Lane. She did not want to leave her group, but this was tangible and Spargo Creek was just too far away. She started to contemplate the prospect of convincing Lowky. He was determined that it was a choice between Spargo Creek or the orphanage.

At least there would be people to talk to, she thought as she turned the last corner before the main street. She had found nothing. She headed back to the base and grabbed some items for trading. She also grabbed some of the excess food they had collected and put it in her pack for emergencies.

Marley had obviously headed back to the market, and the only unchecked area was around and behind the water tanks. Matilda decided to head back that way.

Matilda finally got to the red streak, but Lowky wasn't there. She was furious! She violently threw her pack on the ground, slumped herself on top of it, and cried. She would not do this alone she affirmed.

She stormed to the water tanks, ready to sign up on the spot. The sign-up table was in the area where the water tanks had dried up. There was a line. Matilda listened intently to the people in front of her as she joined the queue.

"Have you checked the family register?" a very tall and skinny woman asked the stumpy girl next to her.

"Not yet, but I checked it yesterday, and it hasn't changed for more than a week."

"Well, you'd better check it again today; they won't sign you up until you've got this." She held up a signature with the date October 7. The date was much later than she and Lowky had calculated.

Silent tears rolled down Matilda's face. Had they really been traveling for so long? She searched back in her memory. Lowky kept all the official dates in his book, but the more Matilda thought about it the move she believed the woman with the stamp was mistaken.

The tall woman spoke again. "Really, Dawn, go get your stamp or you'll just have to line up all over again. I'll try and keep your place in line." Both women casually looked at Matilda, who smiled politely. Then the short one left the line and Matilda quickly followed. She had not heard or seen anything of a family list, but she was uncontrollably filled with hope of finding someone they knew. Alive!

Dawn slowed down a little and glanced over at Matilda. "Did you forget your stamp too?" The lady smiled.

"I didn't even know there was one," Matilda tested.

The woman looked oddly at her. "Have you not checked it yet?" This time her voice was filled with sadness. "Well, good luck. I hope you find someone. There are hundreds of names on the list." She paused. "But if you don't find anyone, you can always come with us."

"Who's us?"

"Oh, we're the singles."

"The singles?" Matilda hesitated. "Who are leaving tomorrow?"

The lady looked at her again, and this time her expression changed and her tone was short. "Where have you been?"

"My family and I got caught on the other side of that," she said, pointing towards the mountain. "We've been lost. We just got here yesterday."

"Where are your family now?"

"Sleeping under a broken wall. My mum is very weak; I am the oldest so she told me to find water," Matilda replied as she watched the women's face for a reaction.

"Well, you came at the right time," she said casually. "This time tomorrow we would have all been gone."

"Gone where?" Matilda queried, trying not to give herself away.

"Well, the families are staying at the stadium about three kilometres away, and it's an easy walk. That's where everything's stored."

"Stored for what?"

"Well, everything. The future!" the lady said curiously. "Look, take this water to your mum, and I'll get you a place in line. When you come back, I'll tell you everything."

Matilda guiltily accepted the water and then moved out of sight.

The woman walked away from the table and through a large group that was gathering nearby. She stopped abruptly and started speaking to three men. Within a few seconds the men all nodded and then walked briskly away from the crowd. Something was wrong; Matilda was sure of it. She raced back to the base, checking over her shoulder at every possibility. Desperately, she hid everything under the semidetached roof and then raced back to market. She stood for a few minutes trying to control her breathing as she walked nonchalantly back up to the woman.

"So what's the family book?" Matilda asked politely as she rejoined the line.

"It's a list of people looking for people. They have matched up over sixty people since we grouped here."

"Where did you all come from?" Matilda asked.

"All over, really. There is about eighty kilometres of area that withheld the earthquake pretty well. Everyone tried to survive and find family, but small groups started to emerge very quickly. Things were starting to get nasty. That radio man—"Reconnection"—have you heard of him?"

Matilda frowned and shrugged.

"Well anyway, he suggested we join together and come up with a plan. He was talking to all survivors, not just us. He said that everyone should just go to the biggest standing building they could get too. Ours was the stadium, and within twelve hours there were four hundred people there. Each day it grew, and now there are almost a thousand people registered."

Matilda nodded politely as the woman continued.

"We are the ones who cleared this area, and the food and supplies we found were stockpiled in the stadium. We've only been eating once a day, at night. The supplies have lasted well, but now they're starting to run low."

"How do you know people haven't been keeping stuff for themselves?" Matilda asked genuinely.

"Everyone is allowed to keep what they can carry. Only the families are staying behind, and they only make up a hundred of the thousand. So there is really no point having more than you can carry."

Matilda nodded as she thought back to the man with the wheelbarrow.

"What about the people who don't want to go?"

"This is a community now; everyone has to follow the rules," the woman said sternly. "People who don't register must move on. Anyone who is in the 'new city' tomorrow needs a family card or they will be removed."

Matilda looked blankly at her.

"I know it's a lot to take in," the lady said kindly, "but we have been working on this since the first stadium meeting."

"Well, what should my family do?" Matilda asked, starting to move away.

The lady grabbed her arm a little too forcefully. "Just wait here and see if anyone else is looking for you," she said, slightly releasing her grip, "and then you can tell your family and register together. It saves having to line up here again."

Matilda looked sceptical.

"Look, there's so many desperate and dying people out there, we have to protect our own."

"Who's running this?" Matilda asked accusingly.

"The SES took over all the details. It was a group decision and they were the only people anyone could trust. Initially the people were suspicious, but as their lives started to improve everyone started to pitch in, and now most of the time we survive pretty well. As you can see, we have done a lot of work, and once we can sustain our own food supply here, we can really start again."

"Who does what?"

"Well, there were so many things to do, so we made a work list. Once you're registered, you are assigned a job. If you don't do that job, then you are deregistered." She smiled. "It's good incentive."

"What do you do?" Matilda asked, still trying to slip out of the woman's grip.

"I'm the 'market coordinator,' so as you can imagine I've been—"

Matilda interrupted. "When is help coming, from the mainland, from the United States? I don't understand why we all haven't been rescued."

"No one really knows." She sighed. "We just know they're not coming. There have been no reported rescues since the fifth day after the quake. Then they just stopped. The helicopters still occasionally fly over with big food creates, but so far we have only seen them drop from the sky. People know were here but . . ."

"But what?"

"Well, from what we've heard—and information is very unreliable—the whole of Australia is damaged. There are only small undamaged pockets, and even those are cut off from everything else. Apparently New Zealand no longer exists due to one of the many tsunamis that the quake caused. Even America and Africa suffered significant damage and loss of life. Everyone is looking after their own." She paused thoughtfully. "And that is what we plan to do."

"How do you know all this?"

"We don't, really. Most of it is guesswork and rumour. We've had scouts searching and returning since we formed, and in the evening they report back. Everything else is decided by a vote; majority rules."

"Wow! I have to tell my family this. We have a lot of very big decisions to make," Matilda said as she started to turn away.

"No, wait," the lady snapped. "While you're here—" The line was now fairly short, with only about ten people in front of them.

"No, I must tell my mother, and we'll all come back together," Matilda said sternly.

"Well, what's your name at least?" the woman said, looking around nervously as her eyes darted from side to side.

"Joanne," Matilda lied. "And yours?"

"Oh, I'm Dawn," she said, extending her hand. "Nice to meet you."

Matilda reluctantly extended her hand. Something was wrong—her stomach told her, her head told her, even the hairs on the back of her neck told her, *Run! Get out of there.* She tried to remove her hand but Dawn gripped it tightly, and this time she was obviously looking for someone.

"Hey, what's up?" Matilda protested as she tried to break free. "Let go!" she screamed.

The people nearby looked around, but as soon as Dawn mouthed *not registered,* they turned away. The three men Dawn had talked to earlier were now heading towards Matilda. Matilda squealed, kicked, and bit, but Dawn refused to let go. In the end, Matilda had no choice; she flipped the woman over her head and into the crowd in front of them.

Chaos ensued as people scrambled to make sense of what had happened. Matilda ran. She ran fast but not straight as she tried everything to lose the men. She noticed they were starting to split up. She would soon be cornered. She jumped into the crumbled plaster of a broken wall and tried to squeeze herself into the gap. She had lost a large amount of weight but wasn't that skinny. She grabbed frantically for a loose bit of plaster as she heard the men's voices getting closer. She tore at the wall next to her. Fanatically she clawed for protection. Her heart pounded so hard and so violently, she thought her eyes would bleed. Her hands were like jelly, and it was a miracle that she managed to hide herself in time.

Once the loud and hostile voices faded away, Matilda realised she had no idea what she was running from. The sun was now low in the sky, and all she wanted was to find Lowky. From the beginning, they had handled these situations together. She headed back to base as quietly and discreetly as she could.

She expected to see nothing, but at least she could recharge and think. As she entered the room she was stunned to find Lowky, Marley, and Chilli all sitting around, clean, dressed, and civilised.

"Coffee anyone?" Chilli smiled.

CHAPTER 25

Blood

"THE market will finish in less than an hour. Is there anything we need?" Lowky interrupted as everyone sat around the fire chatting enthusiastically about the day's events.

"That depends on what we're doing," Matilda said.

"Hadn't we already decided that" Lowky asked curiously. "We have more than we can carry. We leave for Spargo Creek tomorrow. Just as we planned." Lowky looked confused.

"Well, the thing is, Lowky..." Matilda paused and looked at the group, smiling and waiting. "Well, the thing is... oh, it doesn't matter." She smiled happily.

"Okay, well then, do we need anything?"

"Not really; we got everything from the arcade," Matilda replied.

"I think we should trade whatever we want. There's some great stuff out there. Trade anything except food and water." Lowky looked around at a much more presentable crew. "All agreed?"

"Agreed," each replied except for Matilda.

"All agreed, Matilda?" Lowky repeated.

"Yes, but whatever you do, if anyone asks, you have signed up and checked the family register, and you are on your own and leaving tomorrow with everyone else." They waited curiously. "I can't explain now, but trust me on this one." They all nodded politely. "Wait," Matilda snapped. "For God's sake, can we please stay together?"

"What for?" Lowky laughed. "We'll meet back here when were done. It'll save time."

"No," Matilda insisted, but without further information she could not convince them, and within minutes they were all running out the door.

Matilda took longer to get organised. She decided not to trade anything that she couldn't replace. She picked up her first aid kit and took out the spare bandages. Once she was in Spargo Creek she could wash the one she had and reuse it. *This is a safe trade,* she thought responsibly. She kept her walkie-talkie and wondered if Lowky was trading his. They could probably survive with just one. She took it just in case. She searched through her stuff, but all of a sudden everything was precious; she had no extras, no donations for charity. She was the charity, and when she left the base, her day pack was almost empty.

She walked through the market looking for surprises and for the others. Lowky was up ahead in a deep conversation with a man with a screwdriver. The twins were together looking at a half bag of ground coffee.

Matilda stayed at the side, sneaking in and out as something caught her eye. She traded her bandage for a travel pillow, her old jeans for two batteries, and two of her old T-shirts for a pair of oversized walking shoes. She quietly headed back to base and sat silently in her own thoughts until the others returned.

"We thought we'd lost you again." They all laughed as they rolled through the door. Excitedly they started to share their trades. Marley and Chilli had swapped their radio for a wind-up clock and had swapped their percolator for half a bag of coffee. "You still have your percolator, don't you?" Marley asked anxiously.

"Of course." Lowky smiled. He was particularly cheerful and upbeat. "What did you get, Matilda?" he asked warmly.

"Some batteries and some paper and stuff," she mumbled.

"What's wrong with you" Lowky snapped. "Why is there always one person in a bad mood? Can't we have any joy in this godforsaken mess of a place?"

The twins sat shocked, and Matilda just couldn't hold it in any longer.

They all looked at her anxiously as she blurted out everything she had seen and heard. She didn't breathe, she didn't pause, she just opened her mouth and out spilled everything, from her almost signing the register to her hiding in a wall.

"Are you okay?" Lowky asked, shocked.

"Physically, yes, but I feel very shaken."

"Okay," Lowky said. "It's time we made some rules. It's time we decide once and for all what we want from each other. I would like to offer the first rule: we never split up again." He looked at Matilda supportively.

"What if we have to?" Chilli asked sharply.

"Then we stay in twos, and when we get to Spargo Creek we can make new rules, but for now we need structure."

"Okay," the twins said lightly.

"And we never hide food; we share everything," Matilda added.

"Okay," they all agreed.

"Everyone is equal, even Billy," Matilda said.

"What if we are down to our very last meal?" Marley asked.

"Then we split it five ways."

"Okay, agreed," the twins answered.

"I think we need jobs too, based on our skills," Chilli suggested. "Marley and I should be responsible for the meals."

"I'll do the fires and set up the shelter," Lowky suggested.

"I'm not doing the cleaning," Matilda promised. "But I will do all the scouting ahead at the end of the day."

"You and I should share the washing," Lowky said, looking sternly at Matilda.

"I'll do the packing and unpacking and the rationing of food, but I'm not doing the washing," she asserted.

"Fine!" Lowky giggled. "Anything else?"

"Okay, the chores are shared, the scouting is organised, and we all stick together. Agreed?"

They all nodded patiently at Matilda.

Matilda looked deeply into everyone's eyes as she shuffled through her bag. She pulled out her flick knife and cut a deep gash into her thumb. She went to pass the knife to Lowky, but she knew him too well. "Here—give me your hand." She grabbed, and before he knew it Matilda had sliced his thumb. Blood was dripping through his fingers.

"What's this?" the twins asked, confused and disgusted.

"We're a real Tribe now, a family, and families share the same blood. We'll be blood sisters," Matilda said, looking hopefully at Marley.

Lowky put up his thumb, which was now throbbing, and pushed it into Matilda's. Marley nodded bravely, took the knife, and placed it at her thumb. Chilli watched closely, and within a second, Marley had grabbed his hand and sliced randomly. The knife scraped across the back of one of his fingers, and immediately it started to bleed. He sat there speechless as Marley sliced her own thumb and joined it to Matilda's. Chilli held his hand up to Marley for the ritual.

"Not us, silly," she mocked, "you're already my brother."

Once Matilda had finished joining with the others, she pulled out her little black book and wrote up the rules. Then she put a bloodied thumbprint at the bottom and handed it to Lowky to do the same. No one else thought this was necessary, but they sure weren't going to argue with Matilda, not today. At the top of the page she wrote *The Tribe* and then looked at it carefully. She rubbed it out and wrote The Tick Tribe.

Lowky blushed. "Why that?" he asked, flattered.

"Well, you started this stupid adventure, and we need a solid name. Solid like us." She smiled. "Plus it sounds better than the Maya Tribe."

The twins disagreed. "He may have started it, but the Sal-Hencos will never change their name," Chilli responded adamantly.

"We're not naming you, just the tribe." Matilda laughed.

"Well then, why use anyone's name?" Chilli asked.

"Because . . ." Matilda hesitated as she frantically wrote things in her book. "Because . . . the numerology for the Tribe is six, which is a really strong leadership number and is often seen as the dictator number. We need something more democratic, if you know what I mean?"

They all looked at her blankly.

"Clearly not! Anyway, the Tick Tribe is a four, which means fairness and friendship. So it must be the Tick Tribe," she said as she quickly shut her book. "If we're going to do it, we might as well do it properly."

"How's that proper?" Marley snapped.

"Look—" Matilda glared. "You and Chilli became part of the Tribe, but it existed before you and before me. First of all, it was Lowky and Billy—and we're not calling it the Baxter Tribe." Matilda looked at Marley, but she turned away.

Chilli, on the other hand, nodded happily at the explanation and raised his coffee. "To the Tick Tribe."

CHAPTER 26

Attack

Lowky woke up well before dawn, and within minutes everyone was bustling around the fire preparing breakfast. Chilli and Marley were making coffee and preparing bread. Matilda was feeding Billy a luxurious can of dog food, which he breathed in and sat patiently waiting for more. Lowky took a list of inventory so that he could prepare a rations plan.

"Is there enough food for Billy to have another can?"

"Sure," Lowky replied. "As it is we are going to have to leave quite a lot behind.

"Everyone pack your personal day packs, but the big packs have to be for food and water. Does anyone have a plan?"

"Ah, Spargo Creek," Chilli and Marley said in unison."

"Ah, how?" Lowky retorted.

"Well its north, isn't it?"

"Northeast."

"Where do you think we are now?"

"Who knows? Hopefully Sunbury, but probably Bulla." Lowky was now looking intently at the map.

Chilli sat next to him and they both looked confused as they pointed to different places.

"We're about halfway, and it's taken us ages to get this far," Chilli said.

"Nineteen days by my calculations," Lowky said proudly.

"Thirty-six days, according to the market coordinator I met yesterday," Matilda said.

"No, that can't be right!" Marley added. "We calculated twenty-one days."

"Anyway . . ." Chilli waited for everyone to listen. "Anyway, we won't make it another nineteen days on these supplies, so we should head north and look for that supply drop box."

"That's where the 'singles' are going! Maybe we should try and follow them," Matilda added.

"Well, I got nothing else." Lowky smiled, and they all agreed.

Marley looked at her clock. "Its four fifteen a.m. Didn't you say they were leaving at dawn?"

Matilda nodded.

"Well, we'd better get a move on," Marley urged as she downed her coffee and topped everyone's cup. They ate quickly and packed as much as possible. They left behind very little, but what they did leave Lowky stashed carefully in a crevasse beneath some smashed cement.

They walked silently using only a tiny torch, and before long they saw a dim light up ahead. Lowky gestured for everyone to be quiet as they approached a well-beaten shed. They got as close to the window as possible but were not close enough to hear the conversation.

Lowky took off his packs and crept a little closer.

"All right, Abdi, are you ready?" Lowky recognised the silky woman's voice but could not remember her name.

"Ready," he replied.

"And you, Jimmy?"

"Ready."

"Let's do this thing then; let's go."

Lowky could hear the noise of bags being lifted and their last-minute preparations.

He scuffled back to the group and pulled them behind a wall. "There leaving; I think it's just three of them," he whispered.

Matilda was the closest to the edge of the wall. She poked her head out to see a tall blonde lady, packed up to the armpits, and then out came an even taller African man and a small, dumpy, bald guy.

Matilda turned back, smiling. "And I thought we looked bad." She giggled as she looked back around the corner. She had her hand up towards the others, and they stood breathlessly waiting for a sign. From where Matilda was standing the road stretched straight for quite a ways, and she let the strangers get a long way ahead before she turned back to the Tribe.

"Okay, let's go." She smiled as she dropped her hand. The strangers were now small matchbox people on the horizon. The Tribe hurried to keep up and out of sight. They continued like this until finally, as the sun started to set, the strangers came to a stop.

"Thank God!" Matilda whispered. "I'm starving."

"Let's find a spot out of sight," Lowky suggested. "Who wants to scout out what's happening at the adult camp?"

"I will," Matilda replied happily. It was her job after all. She turned around and headed for a well-hidden notch with a great line of sight.

"And who else?"

"You go," Marley insisted. "An Ecuadorian knows how to set up a home."

"It's not a home," Lowky muttered quietly to himself, but he agreed and they decided to meet back in ten minutes. The only landmark they could identify was a standing power pole, a rarity in these parts.

Lowky happily held back as Matilda quietly approached the group. She stayed out of sight and crawled anxiously across the tarmac.

The group spoke loudly, and it wasn't long before she could hear them.

"Great progress, guys; we should be at the car by nightfall tomorrow."

"Were taking a big risk, Abdi" Jimmy angrily replied. "What if the car's not there or the petrol's been taken?"

"Or evaporated, or leaked out?" added the female.

"Hey, it was my trade, and we're still heading north, aren't we? You can go your own way; you didn't have to come with me."

"Sorry, Abdi." The woman interrupted with a soft and warm tone. "Sorry. The car would be a blessing, and it's worth the risk."

"Well, eat wisely and sleep well; we leave before dawn."

Matilda crawled back to Lowky and they both headed to the light pole to find the twins. Chilli was waiting patiently.

"We said ten minutes. Let me check your watch," he said as he grabbed Lowky's hand and shook it vigorously.

"Stop!" Matilda interrupted. "Where's Marley? We've got news."

"At base. I'll take you."

"Why did you split up?" Matilda screamed. "For God's sake, Chilli! Grow up!"

Lowky frantically grabbed Matilda and put his hand over her mouth. "Shhh, Matilda! What are you thinking? Chilli, run!"

Chilli bolted down a small path that had been created by the collapsing structures. This came to an opening that they crossed at lightning speed and then veered under a roof and through a window and they were . . . home!

"What the . . ." Lowky said, accidently out loud.

"How?" Matilda's added predictably.

The room they were standing in had four walls and a fire glowing in the centre. There was the smell of bread and chocolate, and two out of four beds were made.

"Put out the fire! Quickly," Lowky said as he spun back to reality. He threw his only jacket over the top and they sat, like mice, waiting. There was no sound, but the smell of material, slightly smoked, danced slowly through the air. Suddenly there was the sound of feet, like they had dropped directly from the sky.

"Is that the smell of our fire?" the short chubby man known as Jimmy inquired.

"I didn't light it yet," the woman answered curiously.

"Well, I certainly smell fire, don't you?"

There was no answer, but Lowky imagined they were all nodding like bobble-head dolls. Marley started shaking uncontrollably, and Matilda glared at her, trying to will her into silence.

Chilli tried to move to her but Lowky grabbed his leg, and he tumbled noisily to the ground.

"Did you hear that?" Jimmy whispered to the others, and then he yelled, "I hear you!" angrily into the night. "You'd better not breathe 'cause I'll find you . . . where are you? Where are you!" he screamed desperately and then everything went silent; not movie theatre silent, more like haunted house silent.

The air was stiller than Lowky could ever remember. He could see it pulse with every breath. He was determined to pounce when required, to fight. He got ready, on his hands and feet, like a starter in a footrace, but Matilda promptly pulled him back on his arse.

"Idiot," she mouthed as he glared gratefully at her.

"What do you think?" Chilli asked in the smallest whisper.

"This way," screamed the short man and the group came pounding towards the room.

Marley grabbed Chilli's hand, and in one smooth movement jumped through the back window and into what used to be a backyard. Lowky and Matilda followed, but more like "dumb and dumber." They stumbled and slid as the twins coached them from the other side.

"Come on, Matilda, go over the top!"

"Lowky, get your foot around."

It seemed like an hour, but eventually they landed on hands and knees on the other side.

"Run!" Lowky insisted as the adults approached the corner. The Tribe ran, slid, scrambled, and rolled around one corner after another until finally their breath could take them no further. The stopped suddenly and fell down in an exhausted but silent heap.

They lay there so quietly that when it was time to move, both of the twins were fast asleep.

Lowky touched Chilli's shoulder, trying to quietly wake him, but it didn't work. Chilli woke screaming, and both Matilda and Lowky had to jump on him and force him into silence. When they eventually let him free, he was wide-eyed and ready to attack. Everyone sat hoping they had gone unheard, but it was too late, the adults, in all their fury, came charging towards them.

"Run!" Lowky screamed as they all instinctively took hands. Matilda was first in line, and she quickly spotted a gap between two buildings. It was a tight squeeze, but it opened out into a larger area. There they stood, again frozen and shaking.

The area was small and they had to manoeuvre themselves awkwardly onto the ground. Within a few terrifying minutes, they were asleep.

*

The sun was warm and bright on Lowky's face. As usual he woke in a fright, and it took him a while to calm down. *It's okay, you're safe, it going to be a great day.* His heart rate started to slow down. *It's daylight, it's morning. Oh no! The adults, the car! They'll be gone.* His heart rate sped up again. *All is well, Lowky, all is well!* Lowky shielded his eyes with his hand as he moved his head away from the large crack that was letting in the light. The air was filled with dust, and the golden glow was warm and friendly. His heart rate was not. In a flurry he woke Matilda and Marley. This time he let Marley wake Chilli. Matilda started talking, and before long the rest had joined in.

"What time is it?"

"Where are we?"

"Where are the adults?"

"Where's our stuff?"

"*Stop!*" Matilda screamed in her hoarsest, loudest whisper. They looked at her hopefully. "One thing at a time! Marley, what time is it?"

"Seven thirty."

"Okay let's try and find our base. Any complaints, see management." She stormed back out of the tiny gap as quietly as possible.

Finding the road and the base was pretty easy in the daylight. Matilda went in first. She gasped and came rushing back out, almost bumping into Lowky.

"What is it?" Lowky said, annoyed.

"Our stuff—it's gone—they've taken it!"

The room was empty, and only the stunted fire and Lowky's burnt jacket remained.

"We must catch them," he yelled as he stormed back down the road to the area the adults had used as a camp. Lowky could see smoke rising from the top of the structure, and he tentatively approached. He got to within hearing distance and waited. The sky was deep blue and the chill of morning was quickly lifting. Lowky heard nothing, so he slid over a large rock just near the broken window and ducked while he plotted an easy escape. There was still nothing. Lowky took a short silent breath and raised his head so slowly that he looked like a puppet in a boxed theatre. He looked around the camp quickly and then ducked back down with lightning speed. He saw nothing, but he wasn't sure. He bobbed up and down again, but this time he heard the softest of giggles. It was enough to make him spin down and duck with such speed and velocity that he landed on his back.

When he opened his eyes and looked up, he saw a smiling Matilda. She shook her shoulders and put her hand over her mouth to try and contain herself.

Lowky got up grumpily, but this time he moved with much more grace as he tried to shrug off his embarrassment. The room was empty, at least of people.

All of their packs had been taken, but other, less impressive ones stood near the door. The backpack full of water also sat strewn across the floor but mainly intact. They had taken some specialty camping equipment, but apart from that their supplies were almost complete.

Lowky started packing up as Chilli did some investigative work. The fire had been partially covered with dirt but it was still smoking. An old plastic plate lay carelessly at the side. He sniffed it.

"Oh, gee! Eggs! They've got eggs." He touched it with his finger. "Still slightly warm," he muttered. "They've just left, not long, we can catch them."

"Come on!" Marley coaxed, "move it!"

She handed them their day packs and a new one from against the wall. The Tribe moved like a well-oiled machine, except for Chilli, who anxiously grabbed everything from around the room and shoved it wherever it fitted. One by one they were again on their way.

"What's that?" Marley asked after hours of silence. It was nearly dusk, and over the ridge ahead they could see a wisp of rising smoke. "It must be them," she said, lowering her voice to a whisper. "Let's camp here, and no fire. We'll set out scouts when it gets dark enough. Do we still have a torch?"

It took more than two hours to sort out the stuff and write a new inventory list. The items taken of most value were the batteries, the radio, the tarp, and about one day's supply of food. All good stuff too: lollies, nuts, flour, and coffee. What they had gained was much less interesting: some corn flour, baked beans, and a very pale torch. They'd also left some corn chips, which they must have grabbed from the arcade. It was an odd food item because it was fragile and took up lots of space. The Tribe were famished and they agreed on corn chips for dinner. The bag was divided equally, and Billy ate his share without complaint.

"You two stay here; it's our turn to go out," Marley said as she grabbed Chilli's hand and pulled him to his feet.

He looked happily surprised as he wiped off his hands and flashed Lowky and Matilda a cheeky smile.

"Let's walk in the scrub on the side of the road," Chilli suggested, "and Marley, point the torch down!"

"We should really turn it off," she suggested as they comically stumbled and fell through the scrub.

"This is too noisy." Marley giggled as she sifted through her day pack for her reading torch. It let out a tiny light and they followed it like moths. Before long they could smell the fire and what appeared to be cake! They slowed to a snail's pace, getting just close enough to hear the adults talking.

Chilli clumsily stepped on a twig that cracked loudly, and they waited nervously before taking another shaky step. The first thing they heard was laughter. Marley's heart melted and a smile spread across her face as she looked at Chilli. It was too dark to see his face, so she grabbed his hand and led him forward. The laughing subsided as they took another step.

"Pass the pot, please, Joan." It sounded like Abdi, but they were still not close enough to be sure; another step.

"Gee, I'm full," Jimmy said randomly. "It doesn't take much these days."

Marley imagined he was smiling as he said this and wondered how fat he must have been before the quake.

"We made good miles today," Abdi added in a completely unrelated fashion.

"Yeah, where do you think we are?"

The twins heard the shuffling of paper. *They've got a map,* Marley thought.

"No idea," Jimmy said with a laugh. "No really, we've stayed basically north on the same road from Sunbury."

"The C743," Joan chimed in happily as the paper rustled again.

"Yes, well we should be almost in Woodend."

"Really? Great, how far?"

"Well, if I'm correct, about an hour's walk, but it could be ten—depends on the conditions."

"Well, I'm ready," Joan said. "I can't wait to get into that car; I'm sure sick of walking."

They all laughed before falling into a momentary silence.

"The cake is divine, Abdi, just divine."

Marley touched Chilli lightly on the shoulder and his body jumped but his feet stayed on the ground. She grabbed his hand and silently led him away. The further they got the noisier their footsteps became, and before long they felt safe enough to turn their torch back on.

"Wow, Woodend!" Chilli smiled, his cheeks almost bursting with relief. That's way further than we thought, but Lowky was right, I think we're still at least ten days away."

"Yeah, or ten hours with a car!"

"I can't believe they have a car, Marley: that must have been what Matilda was going to tell us last night."

"What?"

"Oh, it doesn't matter. What does matter is that we have a car and the roads have been really good. We could have driven from the plateau." Chilli looked at Matilda, but she wasn't listening.

"Woodend!" she muttered.

"Yeah, it sounds like it," Chilli replied thoughtfully. "Surely there's a way we could use that car to our advantage!"

Lowky was washing his face when the twins returned. "What is it?" he asked immediately.

"The plateau was Sunbury and we're almost at Woodend," Chilli said, still smiling.

"Well, if that's true," Lowky said, "we should be well over halfway to Spargo Creek. I'm sure it's east from Woodend, but I'd have to check the map."

"Weren't the food drops north?" Marley asked.

"We could have passed them already," Matilda said.

"If they even exist," Marley added.

"Did you find out where the adults were heading?" Lowky asked.

"No, they didn't mention it, but we really should follow them to the car. I have a feeling we're going to need it."

"Oh, you heard about the car? I was going to tell you, but what's the point? We can't go up against them," Lowky said rationally.

"But they're not expecting us," Chilli said. "Lowky, we need that car."

"But it's their car."

"Really, Lowky, after what they did to us?"

"They left us food."

"Only because they couldn't carry it!"

"They could have stashed it!"

"Whatever. Maybe we can just hitch a lift, I was thinking..." He paused and thought for a while as Lowky looked proudly at him. "If we could tie the packs to the bumper bar we could grab on ..."

Matilda started laughing; she just couldn't help it.

"Oh, you come up with something." Chilli sulked.

"We could steal the keys," Matilda suggested.

"Are you gonna drive it?" Chilli laughed.

"Well, I was hoping you could." She smiled at him.

"He can, actually," Marley beamed. "He used to drive our uncle's car on the farm in Frankston. It was a beat-up Datsun that nobody could be bothered with. Chilli loved it though. He'd be out there all day long driving in circles."

"Oh, Marley, that was so long ago. Uncle must have sold that farm when I was seven."

"Don't be silly," Marley snapped. "Chilli can drive the car."

"All right, let's not get ahead of ourselves. For now let's just try and keep up. Are they moving any further tonight?"

"No, they're eating cake," Chilli snapped jealously. "They leave in the morning. They're saying the car is an hour away."

Lowky smiled thoughtfully as he leaned back on his bag. *The Tribe couldn't possibly use a car . . . could we?*

CHAPTER 27

Bug

THE all sat perched around the edge of the adult camp, waiting. They were organized; their packs piled up on the side of the road, ready for a quick exit. The darkness was starting to get misty as the sun threatened to rise.

Joan woke first and immediately woke the others.

"Does anyone want coffee?" she asked politely.

"No, I'm eager to get to the car if there is one. Can we have coffee there?"

"Where is the car, exactly?" Jimmy asked.

"On this highway just before Woodend."

"Don't you think it's strange we haven't seen any other cars? This area is pretty undamaged," Joan said.

"My guess is they've all been driven out of here. Anyway, we won't know till we get moving. I want to be on the road today, and who knows what state the car's in!"

The Tribe retreated as the adults packed up their bedding and put out the fire.

Once the adults were a fair way up ahead, the Tribe followed.

The adults suddenly stopped and started laughing.

"What do we do now?" Chilli whispered.

"I'm the scout," Matilda said. "I'll go have a look. If I can get a glimpse of the car we might be able to make a plan."

"I hope it's a truck," Marley mumbled. "That's the only way where going anywhere!"

Matilda was still a fair distance from the adults when she heard Abdi scream. The anger and volume of his voice made her jump and she scurried backward out of fright.

"*There is no key!*" he screamed. "*They said there was a key!*"

Matilda gathered her courage and moved closer. She heard Abdi throw his body against the metal of the car and start to sob. For the first time since the adults had chased them through the night, Matilda felt sorry.

"There are no keys," she announced to the others as she dramatically returned to the circle.

"We know," Lowky said, "we heard."

"There must be keys. when the adults leave, we'll look for them," Chilli said.

"No, we should follow the adults, at least tilL we get some more supplies."

"Please? can't we just look at the car?" Chilli said stubbornly.

"It probably wouldn't have started," Lowky said reluctantly. "what sort of car was it, anyway?"

"I don't know. It was yellow," Matilda said.

"Really?" Lowky said, annoyed. "What sort of scout are you?"

"Okay, it was round and little with little lights. Like the one in the photo with your mum. You know, the one in the hallway at your house, that white car, like that!"

"A Volkswagen? A Beetle? A Bug?" Lowky said as he jumped to his feet and hugged Matilda.

"I don't know." She shrugged.

"I can start that car!" He grinned. "I can start it without a key!"

CHAPTER 28

Ignition

THE Tribe patiently sat in the bushes as the adults scoured the area for keys. The longer they looked, the louder they became.

Finally Abdi surrendered. "This car is useless to us. We might as well move on."

"Move to where, Abdi?" Joan snapped. "We've probably passed the food drops."

"Where were we going to drive to anyway?" Jimmy asked, defeated. "We never really had a plan; we should have stayed with the others."

"Well, I'm going to walk till I find something," Abdi snapped as he picked up his pack.

"Find what exactly?" Jimmy asked.

Abdi ignored him and started walking up the road. Joan reluctantly followed, and finally so did Jimmy.

Marley immediately started collecting wood for a fire. They had been keeping a low profile and had avoided lighting one while they followed the adults.

"Oh, gee!" she almost squealed. "Coffee, anyone?"

"Yes, please," they all said as a smile spread through the camp.

"I'm going to have a look at the car," Lowky announced hopefully. "Anyone coming?"

"I will!" Matilda laughed. "'Cause we all know, an Ecuadorian knows how to set up a home."

*

The car was exactly like the one his mum had owned. It was a bomb really, but Lowky had loved it. Every trip in that car was an adventure. None of the doors opened, so they would have to climb in through a permanently open window. Once they were inside, Lowky used to sit above a hole in the floor about the size of a small pizza. He used to ride in the car transfixed as the bitumen flew past underneath. His legs would ache as his feet hovered precariously above the hole, just in case the entire floor caved in. Lowky would sit in the back and watch through the gap between the door and the driver's seat as his mum fiddled with the wires under the dash just to get the car started—there was no key! Eventually as the car chugged, his mum would hit the accelerator and the journey would begin.

Lowky was sure he could start this car. "Matilda, we have to check the petrol tank first. There is absolutely no point if there is no petrol."

"Okay," she replied as she moved around the car. The car had a fair bit of cosmetic damage, and the petrol cap was missing. Matilda grabbed a stick and shoved it inside. When she pulled it out, the stick dripped with liquid gold.

"Lowky, its got petrol!" She laughed. "It's got heaps of petrol."

"Great!" he replied as he jumped in to the driver's seat and looked for the panel under the dash. The wires were a little different from his mum's, and he tried desperately to remember what she used to do. *Was it the two black wires? Was it the black and the blue wire? It definitely wasn't the red wire . . . or was it?*

Lowky pulled at two black wires until he found the ends. He nervously attempted to touch them together, but he jumped before they actually did. He tried again. This time they touched for a microsecond, but nothing happened. Lowky tried one final time with more confidence and determination, but even when he held the wires firmly together, there was nothing.

Okay it's not the black ones. He was sure that one of the wires his mum used was black, so he kept one and then yanked at a blue wire until it released itself from the console. He touched the ends and screamed as the car churned, jumped, and then abruptly stopped.

"Oh my God, Matilda, I think it's going to start!" Lowky said, looking towards her. Lowky tried again, this time more prepared for a reaction. The wires touched and the car sprang to life. Lowky tried desperately to keep the wires together but the car jerked forward and stopped as abruptly as it had the time before. Lowky repeated this procedure numerous times before he hit his head against the steering wheel in sheer frustration. The horn beeped.

Marley and Chilli had heard the car turn over a few times and thought the horn was a signal for them to come over. They both scooped up their coffees and headed optimistically towards the car.

Lowky tried one final time, but the car predictably jerked to a violent stop. In complete disbelief, Lowky almost hit his head on the roof when Chilli's face appeared at the window. "Shit, Chilli, what are you doing? I thought you were making a fire."

"You're the one who honked the horn." He smiled. "Anyway, you'll never start a manual like that, you don't even have your foot on the clutch."

Lowky looked blankly at him.

"Here, I'll get in and you start the car," Chilli said as Lowky happily exchanged places with him.

"Ready?" he asked. Chilli manoeuvred himself until he had one foot on each of the pedals.

"Ready!" he replied. "Fingers crossed."

"One . . . two—" Lowky looked hopefully up at Chilli. "Three!" He touched the wires while Chilli pumped the accelerator.

The car chugged . . . the car spluttered . . . and all of a sudden the car was driving down the road. Chilli was whooping with delight as all the others cheered him down the road. Billy nipped at the tyres as he barked supportively.

Chilli stopped the car a few metres up the road and sat casually with his arm hanging out the window. The car idled smoothly as he waited for the others to approach.

"Get our stuff!" He smiled. "The metre's running."

Lowky, Matilda, and Marley ran back to the fire, all laughing and talking at once. They stopped for only a second to chug the warm, sweet coffee Marley had made earlier. They hobbled, overloaded with luggage back to the car and laughed and joked as they somehow managed to pile everything in.

"Ready!" Chilli said proudly as he shifted the gear stick into first, turned left, and started driving towards Spargo Creek.

CHAPTER 29

Highway

BILLY sat happily on Lowky's lap with his head out the window and his tongue flapping back and forth. Marley and Chilli sat in the front chatting rapidly in a mixture of English and Spanish. Marley looked around the car, smiling uncontrollably.

"What is it?" Matilda asked curiously.

"You know what we need?" Marley smiled. "Pass me my day pack and I'll show you."

Matilda scrambled around the back until she found it and then glanced suspiciously at Marley. The pack was lighter than Matilda had remembered, and it swung wildly back and forth as she tried to pass it through the centre console. Chilli ducked as it narrowly missed hitting him in the head.

"Hey, watch it!" he said smartly. "I'm trying to drive."

Marley smiled as she shuffled through her bag and bought out half a packet of crackers left over from dinner the night before.

"Is that it?" Matilda asked sharply as she grabbed the crackers out of Marley's hand. "Really, Marley, you had me excited over nothing," she said as she placed a cracker in her mouth and handed the box to Lowky.

Matilda was gazing out the window when Marley said, "So you don't want any of this then?"

Matilda barely had a chance to look up when Lowky snatched a jar of Mr. Sal-Henco's pickles out of Marley's hand and started examining the label.

"Toasted avocado candy in a sweet potato and burnt liquorice sauce." Everyone looked up at him in anticipation. "Can I have some?" he asked politely.

"Of course." Marley smiled as Lowky plunged a cracker into the jar and then sat back mesmerised as the sweet, silky concoction coated his thoughts and stomach with pure joy.

Lowky deliriously handed the jar to Matilda, but Chilli insisted he should be next if he was to continue driving.

Lowky composed himself and started looking for his map as the others had their turn with the jar. It took him ages to unfold as it had ripped and separated in several places. It was well worn, and Lowky wondered for a second what they would have done without it. He scanned the map and easily found Spargo Creek; then he traced his finger back looking for Woodend. He stopped and looked at the map again. His face turned white and a tear splashed the map.

He finally composed himself and cleared his throat to get the attention of the Tribe. "Um, from the look of it"—he took a very deep breath before continuing—"anyway, from the looks of things we should be in Spargo Creek in about an hour!"

At first everyone cheered and asked questions and started making plans, but then, as if by magic, everyone stopped talking and the car went deadly silent.

Chilli drove smoothly but it appeared that he had dramatically slowed. Matilda gazed out the window, one arm stretched across the back seat to stroke Billy. She never moved her head though; she just stared quietly at the scenery. Lowky cried; like Matilda, he was looking out the window and the tears flowed rapidly as he tried to control his breathing.

The scenery passed in a blur until he and Chilli both spotted a sign saying Welcome to Spargo Creek. Chilli suddenly stopped the car and jumped out, running to the sign, yelling, "We made it! We made it!"

The girls, who had no idea what was going on, looked towards Lowky, but he was already out of the car and hugging Chilli in a dance of victory.

When the boys had finally stopped jumping, they managed to point to the sign, and the girls both collapsed on the ground, laughing and crying in each other's arms.

It wasn't long before the Tribe were all lying on the ground staring thankfully up at the sky. Lowky watched a lonely cloud pass over as he tried to remember where the property was. He had only ever thought about getting to Spargo Creek, and it became painfully obvious he had no idea where to go next. He tried conjuring up old memories, but nothing seemed familiar. What he did remember was that the house number was eighteen. He remembered because the fence to the property was made up of thousands of local rocks and the house number had been set into the fence using deep red clay from the area behind the dam. On one of their visits it had been Lowky and Ales's job to collect buckets of red clay and bring it to the fence to be shaped into stones.

Lowky confronted the Tribe about his concerns, and they all stood around the sign trying to come up with ideas. He looked at them gratefully as they calmly and strategically planned their next move.

Marley suggested they try and find the main street and cook up some dinner, and maybe Lowky would remember something there. Everyone agreed, as it had been an exhausting day, and a few more hours on the road weren't going to make any difference now.

They all got back into the car and started driving to what the sign had suggested was the town centre. As they approached, Matilda and Marley started singing "I Feel Good" by James Brown as Chilli tapped his fingers on the steering wheel. The road curved and twisted and the countryside was exactly as Lowky had remembered. He started thinking of the kookaburra that used to wake him every morning and wondered if it still lived there. Suddenly Chilli hit the brakes and they all went flying towards the windscreen.

"What are you doing?" Marley screamed as she peeled herself off the dash.

"Don't blame me," he snapped. "Have a look at the road!"

The road was dusted with some large rocks, and then it crumbled into a significant split about three metres wide. Lowky scoured the area looking for a way around, but it was useless. They would have to abandon the car and move ahead on foot. The other side of the split was uneven and damaged and seemed to disintegrate the closer it got to town. Their hearts sank, but they managed to unpack the car and cross the split without too much trouble.

Once on the other side, they could see the area had been badly damaged, and they imagined there was an even bigger split ahead. Lowky thought the property must have been on the other side of the main street, which was still at least three kilometres away.

He looked to the left to try and find an easier way to get to town. They were standing about halfway up a small mountain, and Lowky could see across the valley to the hill on the other side. Lowky's eye was immediately drawn to a flash of red. His heart started to pound. He searched the area near the red and saw a small silver dot that looked like a roof.

"Come on!" Matilda said, who had stopped so Lowky could catch up.

Lowky ignored her, and she started walking towards him to see what he was looking at. "What is it, Lowky? Come on, I'm starving. We've hardly eaten anything all day!"

Lowky grabbed Matilda by the arm and pulled her toward him. "Look at that, Matilda—do you see that red spot?" he asked, pointing towards the horizon.

"Yes," she replied as she followed his finger with her eyes.

"Is that a roof to the left?"

"It looks like it; it's hard to tell from here."

"Do you think that's water at the front, like a dam?" he anxiously added.

"It could be, Lowky, but we still have plenty of water. Come on!"

"No, Matilda, you don't get it! That's it! At least I think that's it. I think that's Isaac's bus," he said pointing to the red spot again.

"Isaac! The guy who owns the property? Is that . . ."

"Yes, Matilda, I'm sure of it. That's his bus and the shed," he said pointing to the silver spot, "and if that's water, then that's where his dam would be."

"You're joking, aren't you?" Matilda asked.

"No, I'm not," he said kindly as a smile and tears simultaneously engulfed his face.

"Marley! Chilli! He's found it! Stop! He's found it! We made it!" Matilda screamed ahead, "Marley, Chilli, we're here!"

CHAPTER 30

Houdini

E LATION floated over the Tribe as they headed down the mountain into the valley below. They decided that there was no point looking for a road as everything in front of them was significantly damaged. To the left, the landscape was more intact, but it meant leaving the road and travelling through rugged bush terrain. The red spot was across the valley and about halfway up the hill on the other side. Lowky struggled to estimate the distance but he guessed it was more than three kilometres but fewer than ten.

They grabbed their packs and stepped off the road. The scrub was thick, and they often had to go around dense areas. They spoke happily as they focused on their footing. Lowky had forgotten about being hungry until Marley stopped and pulled out the crackers from her pack.

"Oh great, I'm starving," Matilda said as she rudely snatched the biscuits.

"Should we stop and eat?" Chilli asked hopefully.

"Oh, I don't think I could stop," Lowky added. "Not now, Chilli—I couldn't!" He stopped and looked at the others. "Please! We're so close, can't we eat and walk? I've got some smoked oysters, I'm sure of it."

"Yeah, let's walk," Matilda said forcefully. "I can't wait another second. Aren't you curious, Chilli?"

"Yeah, I'm curious, but I'm starving!"

"You're not starving, Chilli," Lowky muttered. "Look, there's still a packet of snakes; we can eat some of those," he said as he threw the packet to Chilli.

"Okay." Chilli surrendered as he shoved one into his mouth. "Do you want one, Billy" he said happily as the sweet sugary lolly slid down his throat.

"Not too much, Chilli" Lowky warned. "We have no idea what where going to find there. There may be nothing to eat, so we still have go easy."

"What? It's not long till dinner, Lowky, and we haven't even had breakfast or lunch for that matter, so we're eating these snakes! Okay!"

"Okay, Chilli." Lowky laughed as he grabbed them and divided them into five.

The red spot remained visible for a while, but it wasn't long before they were under a canopy of trees and couldn't see it anymore. They had used their compass to check the direction and now they just had to have faith that they wouldn't miss it. The laughter and preparation soon turned to a few odd words as they waited for the property to magically appear. They had long ago crossed the valley floor and were now heading up the hill on the other side.

"It can't be far," Lowky whispered. "What if it's not his property?"

"It's better than nothing, and at least it's a place to rest. It has to be something!"

"Maybe we've passed it," Chilli said flatly.

"I doubt it. We've been following the compass. It was a fair way up this hill."

"Do you think Isaac will be there?" Matilda asked timidly "It's his property after all."

"Doubt it," Lowky said casually.

"Lowky, we have to consider that he probably won't want four kids and a dog just turning up and eating all his food."

"It's okay, Matilda, don't worry. Anyway, it would be great if Isaac was there. That would mean that the chickens have been feed and the gardens are being looked after. Plus, when I was here last time, there was more than enough food on the property. I'm sure it will be fine; he's known my mum for years." Lowky tried to sound convincing, but he really had no idea what Isaac would say. In all the times that Lowky had been to Spargo Creek, Isaac had only been there once. He was always away on business. If Lowky remembered correctly, the man made fireworks. "I really don't think he'll be there," Lowky added as they walked over a small ridge and past a fence.

"Oh my God." Lowky beamed. "This is it! I helped make that fence." Lowky didn't wait for the others; he jumped the fence and started running through the waist-high grass.

"Wait up!" Matilda screamed.

"This is it, Matilda! It can't be far; come on."

He had never followed the fence all the way around the property, so he had no idea how far back it went. His heart pounded as he raced forward. He passed a massive tree that somehow looked familiar. He turned to look at it and fell backward over . . . a chicken! He looked again, twice! He laughed out loud as the chicken disappeared into the scrub and then popped back out again.

"Grab it!" Lowky chuckled as he tried to get up and compose himself.

Matilda looked at him curiously and shrugged. "The chicken, Matilda, grab it!"

"Oh right!" she said as she spotted the bird and leapt forward. She had super-fast reflexes but the chicken was faster, and she landed face first in the dirt. That was it; Lowky couldn't take it anymore, he fell back to the ground, laughing hysterically.

Marley tried next, but the chicken just looked at her and turned back towards Lowky.

"Quick, go that way!" Lowky pointed to Chilli. "We'll try and cut her off."

"I'll come around the back," Matilda whispered as she gestured towards Marley to do the same. Billy stayed with Matilda and barked enthusiastically. They all circled the chicken and slowly started moving in.

"One . . . two . . . three," Lowky whispered as they all jumped towards the chicken, missing her completely and landing in an awkward pile. The chicken scurried off into the bushes, untouched. They all looked ridiculous and burst into laughter as they tried to get up.

"Come on!" Lowky laughed. "Let's follow her."

They dusted themselves off and one by one followed the chicken back into the bush.

"There she is." Matilda pointed as they all ran toward her. The bird moved swiftly, ducking and weaving as the Tribe tried to corner her. Matilda started to chase her around a pocket of trees, but Lowky stopped dead in his tracks. In front of him was Isaac's bus!

The bus was just as Lowky remembered it: old and rusty. It originally sat up on large grey Besser Blocks, but the earthquake must have shifted it, and it now lay with its base flat on the ground. Some of the Besser Blocks remained underneath and it seesawed precariously from side to side. The engine and the wheels of the bus had been removed long before Lowky had ever gone to the property, and the bus was mainly used as a guest room.

The Tribe just stood there looking at it until Chilli finally broke the silence. "Hey, does this place have any food?"

CHAPTER 31

○

Home

Lowky started walking towards the garden as he had done so many times before with Ales. Matilda was collecting firewood, and the twins where setting up *home*. It was dusk, and night was fast approaching. Lowky felt the exhaustion of the day wash over him like a shower. Then he felt the emotion of the journey bombard him like a thunderstorm. He breathed calmly as he confirmed that he *was not* going to eat one more meal without vegetables.

The path to the garden was overgrown, and to the left Lowky could see the chicken hutch, which was large enough to house a small family. The hutch had been damaged in the quake but it remained standing, and Lowky watched gratefully as three hens made their way through the door. The veggie patch was also terribly overgrown, and it was clear Isaac hadn't been on the property since before the quake.

Lowky walked optimistically towards what looked like a carrot top. He gently pulled at it, and up popped three beautiful baby carrots. He immediately dusted one off and put it into his mouth. It was the sweetest thing he had ever tasted. He felt every cell in his body dance with excitement and he did a little dance too. He pulled up another bunch and placed them in a basket he'd made out of his jumper.

As he looked around the garden, vegetables started to appear out of the undergrowth, and before long he had filled his jumper with spring onions, beans, strawberries, and spinach.

On the way back to the bus, Lowky stopped at the chicken hutch and found twelve hens inside. It was nothing compared to the amount he remembered, but it was more than enough for them. He gently reached under one of the birds, but it angrily pecked him, and he had to shoo it away. He found at least twelve eggs under that hen, but he didn't know how long they'd been there so he took the two warmest ones and went to the next nesting box. Each box was full to the brim with eggs, and it wasn't long before Lowky had eight warm eggs placed carefully in his jacket pockets.

He arrived back at the bus after what he thought was only a few minutes. As usual he was amazed. The twins had already straightened up the bus and had made four beds inside with fresh sheets and blankets they had found in the shed. A small fire was blazing, and Lowky could smell bread cooking and coffee brewing. Matilda came back from behind the bus with her arms full of firewood.

"How do they do it?" she asked Lowky, but he just shrugged and sat in a camp chair by the fire. They all came over to see what he had found.

"Oh my God, vegetables." Matilda giggled happily as she searched through Lowky's collection. Marley grabbed the carrots and immediately started cooking.

Lowky looked around at the still dirty and dishevelled Tribe and couldn't have been happier. He watched Billy jump up on to Matilda's lap, and she patted him warmly. Chilli was washing his hands in some warm water, and Marley was smiling profusely as she cracked the eggs into a sizzling pan.

Lowky lifted his head to watch a slowly rising crescent moon. He took a deep breath, shut his eyes, and listened as his little internal voice whispered . . . *All is well.*

ABOUT THE AUTHOR

Erika Logan was born in Melbourne and raised in Adelaide. She returned to Melbourne at age eighteen to study writing and editing at RMIT. She spent ten years as a youth worker and currently teaches primary school at an inner-city school in Melbourne's north.

She lives with her partner, a dog named Buddy Buster (the inspiration for Billy Baxter in the book), and two cats.